LIFE ON THE GUEST LIST

By Laurel Federbush

This is a work of fiction, inspired but by no means limited by reality.

Cover illustration by the author.
Photo by Michael Hough.

Printed in Victoria, Canada

National Library of Canada Cataloguing in Publication Data

Federbush, Laurel
Life on the guest list / Laurel Federbush.
ISBN 1-4120-0027-0
I. Title.
PS3556.E242L53 2003 813'.54 C2003-901594-7

TRAFFORD

This book was published *on-demand* in cooperation with Trafford Publishing.
On-demand publishing is a unique process and service of making a book available for retail sale to the public taking advantage of on-demand manufacturing and Internet marketing. **On-demand publishing** includes promotions, retail sales, manufacturing, order fulfilment, accounting and collecting royalties on behalf of the author.

Suite 6E, 2333 Government St., Victoria, B.C. V8T 4P4, CANADA
Phone 250-383-6864 Toll-free 1-888-232-4444 (Canada & US)
Fax 250-383-6804 E-mail sales@trafford.com
Web site www.trafford.com TRAFFORD PUBLISHING IS A DIVISION OF TRAFFORD HOLDINGS LTD.
Trafford Catalogue #03-0389 www.trafford.com/robots/03-0389.html

10 9 8 7 6 5 4 3

This novel was inspired by the fascinating musicians connected with the Pukka Orchestra, particularly ace guitarist Neil Chapman. I dedicate this book to them and to their fans. – L.F.

CHAPTER 1

I want to tell you about my group — my idols, my heroes, my friends. I'm telling this story because I was there and it mattered, and if I don't tell it, I'm afraid it will be lost and discarded, like a torn-up old poster for some long-past gig.

* * *

That first winter in Toronto was beastly. 1985 — monster snowdrifts, arctic winds blasting from every street corner, all combined to persecute me in this frigid city nearly three hundred miles from my Michigan home.

I was lonely in Toronto, desperately lonely. Barely recovered from anorexia, and on the brink of failing most of my classes at the Faculty of Music, I practiced the harp, my major, mainly out of fear of an implacable teacher and a slew of tyrannical conductors.

Most evenings, I ended up in the basement of the Edward Johnson Building to practice. It always amazed me that I could spend so much of my time in this place and yet feel no connection to it whatsoever. Sterile, antiseptic, and empty, the interior of the modern concrete building seemed to reflect the teaching philosophy of the school.

My heart would sink every time I entered the harp practice room for my self-imposed period of solitary confinement. One of the other harp students had put in a small lamp and an old-fashioned chair in a pathetic attempt to make the room look hospitable; instead, they accentuated its bleakness.

Taking frequent breaks in my practicing, I would seek refuge in my Walkman. The pop and rock tunes beating through my headphones spoke to me of exhilaration and life. I would switch back and forth among Q107, CFNY, and CHUM, the last of which was broadcast from the CN tower, that giddy symbol of hope rising over the city. It gave me some comfort to think of the great tower communicating with me in this personal way. Entombed as I was down here, the city hadn't forgotten me.

Near midnight, when the building was about to close, I would emerge from its bowels and re-enter the world. Cold air rushing into my lungs, the car noises and bright lights of Bloor and Avenue Road bombarding me, I felt like someone coming out of sensory deprivation.

* * *

As a student, I generally stuck to the campus, centered in stern-looking buildings around Bloor Street and St. George, and blending into the wooded, residential area called the Annex.

But Toronto had other areas, places that seemingly appeared as I entered them and disappeared as I left: Yonge Street, the heart of the city; the pungent stretch of Dundas called Chinatown; trendy Queen Street West; and Yorkville, the ritzy area with palm readers and buskers.

Far away, existing only as a vague rumor, lay the eastern end of Queen Street known as the Beaches.

All of this terrain was guarded by the mighty CN Tower to the south; and Casa Loma, the fairytale-like castle on the hill, to the north. Streetcars coasted through, to and from phantom corners of the city; and distant skyscrapers floated mysteriously above it all.

Below, the cool, sleek subways became my personal underground railroad to freedom. Subway stations, in general, were spartanly bare, although a few were tiled with colorful mosaic designs. Cold and impersonal, they still seemed a luxury, a thrill, a sort of amusement park ride that hinted at excitement just around the bend. Trains whooshed by, on their way to and from miraculous places. I could hop on one and go anywhere. Most of the time, though, I didn't. There was always practicing, and the futile studying for my theory classes. Sometimes I would escape downtown on a specific errand, but usually I ended up back here, at the Museum subway stop, in front of the Edward Johnson Building; or at the Spadina stop, near the Annex co-op where I lived.

Although I had a harp in my room, I rarely practiced there, out of deference to my roommate, a psychology major from Sarnia. We got along well enough by staying out of each other's way. My life at the co-op was purely functional; I ate and slept there. Since I was a vegetarian in a meat-eating house, my meals generally consisted of cereal, yogurt, or peanut-butter-and-jelly or cheese sandwiches that I scraped together from the foodstuffs kept in the cavernous pantry. This place fed roughly a hundred people, whom I could hear laughing and joking in line in the dining room while I foraged in back for scraps, peering out from beneath a mess of brown hair, as furtively as a rodent.

Mainly, I subsisted on apples. I ate tons of them, five or six a day. Matsu, Japanese pear-apples, ordinary red delicious, always the biggest ones I could find. When money became a problem, I would buy the reduced-priced, bruised apples, all wrapped together in plastic, with "39c" written in black magic marker on the front. But I needed those apples. They were sweet, they filled me with energy — and they had no fat. I gorged on apples, feasted on apples. They made me feel nourished and satisfied, while in reality I was eating practically nothing at all.

* * *

Once my brother had come to visit and, alarmed at what a hermit his sister had become, had dragged me out to a local nightclub called the El Mocambo. They had advertised for that night a rock band that was getting lots of airplay: the Sandalmen.

Seating ourselves at a table in the packed room upstairs, we ordered beers and drank in the tuneful songs served up by the band, a couple of which I had heard before on my Walkman, in stolen moments of freedom from practicing.

It was the first time I had ever been in a bar, and I had assumed that it would be a sleazy experience. To my great surprise, it ended up being my first really good time since arriving in Toronto.

Later I bought a copy of the band's record, and I would listen to it on my phonograph when my roommate was out. I soon fell in love with the singer's nasal, Scotland-tinged warble. *"Girl beside the rubber tree..."* Laird Jamison's languid voice brought me solace. I began to enjoy living here. Perhaps I would meet him.

The record jacket had a wavy-lined drawing of a mermaid with flowing hair and round, hypnotic eyes. I would often gaze into those eyes, hoping that I might fall into them, into some magical world of enchantment.

Returning to Toronto after midterm break, I was shocked to read in the local papers that Laird had taken ill on a trip home to Glasgow, and would remain there awaiting a kidney transplant.

The city lights darkened for me. Again I was alone.

* * *

My practicing regimen at the Edward Johnson Building continued. Once a guy to whom I had nodded in the hall a couple of times asked me out. Later I found myself on a shabby couch in his apartment, fighting off his clumsy attempts to grope me.

Stammering my apologies, I left the apartment. A heated argument was going on down the hall, and I escaped in the other direction down a stairway.

Since the area was unfamiliar to me, I made my way toward the city noises of the nearest main road, which turned out to be Queen Street. From there I planned to find a bus or streetcar or subway stop. Tattered posters fluttered from the lampposts and building walls.

One of the posters caught my eye. It mentioned a gig at a place called the Serpent's Plume, whose address, I deduced from the number, was not far away. Playing there, the poster advertised, were a singer named Ruby Treece and, in her band, Mink Lasher, the guitarist from the Sandalmen. What a strange night this had become!

I found the club on the upper floor of a restaurant. After mounting a seemingly endless staircase, I straggled in.

Except for the bartender and a handful of people sitting on stools at the bar, apparently oblivious to the music, the place was empty. Even so, at the far end of the room, a band was going at full blast. I located myself at a table to the side, as inconspicuous as I could be in the deserted room, and hungrily observed the musicians onstage.

There, standing partly in shadow, was Mink Lasher, with a red scarf thrown loosely about his neck, sweating over a black speckled guitar, his hand striking the instrument in a fierce strumming motion. A petite blonde woman whom I assumed to be Ruby Treece stood at the front of the stage, in a black mini-skirt and gray beret, her misty voice lyrical against the stormy accompaniment of the band. At one point Mink stepped forward into the light and, as if possessed by some invisible spirit, broke into an eerie, fantastically complicated and yet beautiful solo. I had seen him play once before, but not from this close. Eyes shut, perspiration beaded on his brow, he winced like one in agony, even as his fingers slid effortlessly over the strings. I became aware of an intense physical sensation, as if there were a forcefield around him that might draw me in.

Ruby came back to the microphone, nodding with admiration at Mink as he receded into the background. "*Dancing across a tightrope...*" There was the chorus again, with its simple and yet haunting melody. I was completely entranced, forgetting to clap after the three unison chords that marked the end of the song.

"Oh no, someone's actually listening to us," Mink quipped from the stage.

Despite his words, and the fact that I was the only person in the audience, I knew they weren't playing for me. Still, I felt myself blushing.

Taking a break after another two songs, the band members arranged themselves around a table. For a while I sat where I was, but gradually my curiosity made up for my lack of courage. I had to approach them.

I edged closer until I was only a couple of feet from Mink's black t-shirted shoulder, hoping he would notice me and at the same time hoping he wouldn't. He was studying a picture, his lips pursed with solemnity. Eventually he turned his head slightly and, seeing me there, looked up, a bit startled.

I struggled to speak, and the words sputtered out: "I...really like your music."

"Thank you. Thank you very much," he replied. His gaunt, dark-browed face, set with slightly crooked teeth, brightened into an oddly youthful smile.

"Just thought I'd come over and..." my voice trailed off into a mumble.

"What's that?" he asked.

"N-nothing." With that I retreated to my seat. I remained there, heart pounding, blood rushing again to my down-turned face, until the next set began.

* * *

That May, when my first year at the U. of T. came to an end, my family came to collect me, my harp, and all of my sloppily-packed suitcases and boxes. I had always welcomed summer vacation, but this particular one found me in Ann Arbor longing to be five hours east.

Returning in late August, I saw Ruby's name in the fine print of *NOW Magazine's* club listings. Apparently she was scheduled to play at the Horseshoe, one of Queen Street's more prominent clubs.

I walked the three miles or so from my co-op to the club through the crisp air, feeling that each step I took along the noisy Spadina sprawl was more important than anything I had done in ages.

At last reaching the club, I passed through the somewhat intimidating front room that was dominated by a bar and pool tables, and following the siren song of an electric guitar being tuned, went on back to the room where the band was to play.

As before, the place was virtually empty, but then again I was early. An hour early, it turned out. I situated myself near the front, yet to the side, again trying to be inconspicuous, pulling a paperback book out of my oversized purse and starting to read, as if I had no abnormal interest in what was going on onstage and no inordinate awe for the people up there.

Someone approached me from behind. "I remember you!" Ruby, smiling warmly, pulled up a chair next to me and sat down. "I'm Ruby," she said, as if she needed to introduce herself.

Wobbling the table in my haste, I moved aside to make room for her. "I'm Iris."

"You were at that club upstairs of...wherever it was. That was a freaky place! I won't be going back, that's for sure!" Almost skeletally thin, and yet vibrantly alive, she seemed a strange sprite of a woman. Surrounded by the faintest of crow's feet, her eyes sparkled in the dim light of the club.

"Your songs have been going through my head since that night. They're incredible!"

"Thank you!" She beamed, as if heartened by my lame compliment. "I'm happy to hear that." She noticed my book. "So, what are you reading?"

I handed her my book, whatever it was.

"It looks interesting." She took it in her tiny, fine-boned hands and perused the cover.

I was flattered that she approved.

"So, are you a musician, or what do you do?" she asked.

"I'm a music student at the University of Toronto. I play the harp."

She looked impressed. "The harp! That must be such a joy to play! You're truly blessed."

The joy of playing had long eluded me, but sitting there with Ruby I did indeed feel blessed.

"We'll be playing at the Silver Dollar on September eighteenth. I can put you on the guest list." She chuckled. "The club gives me more money if I can get a lot of people on the guest list to come. Can I take down your phone number?"

As she reached into her velvet, ornamental purse for a pen, I struggled to remember even one of the seven digits.

The rest of the night saw me slightly tipsy, somewhat giddy, and totally in heaven.

* * *

Every day I scrutinized my mail for Ruby's invitation to the gig in September. The fact was that I had no understanding of what she had meant by a "guest list," and I supposed that it must include some kind of special ticket that she would send me. Although I couldn't remember doing so, I must have given her my address. As the date approached, I despaired that she must have forgotten me. It had all been too good to be true.

On the evening of the eighteenth, as I sat on my littered floor, eating from a bowl of raisin bran as I mentally prepared myself for the event, the phone rang. I set the bowl down and crawled across the room to answer it.

A foggy woman's voice asked: "Hello, is this Iris?"

"Yeah."

"Iris, this is Ruby speaking. Just reminding you that we'll be at the Silver Dollar tonight, and I'm putting your name on the guest list, if you want to come." There it was, her magical voice, glowing and fluorescent. I found it hard to believe that something as ordinary as my telephone could contain it.

"Of course I'll be there!" I practically shrieked.

"All right then. Just give them your name at the door, and...I'll see you later."

We both hung up and I sat there for a while, trembling.

CHAPTER 2

Ruby's performances became the mainstay of my Toronto existence. I would feverishly scan the club listings for her gigs. They didn't happen often, but once in a while her band would play at Grossman's Tavern three nights in a row. I would always make it a point to go two out of the three nights; if I went every night, they might think I was obsessive.

Smoky and run-down, the working-class joint at Spadina and College seemed a palace to me, exalted by the presence of the musicians within. Each time I would enter the club only after much hesitation, but somehow Ruby always treated me like an old friend. During breaks she would come over and sit beside me, chatting about the evening's sets and inquiring about my studies. Sometimes it was only for a minute, but well long enough for her to envelop me in her mysterious charm.

And always at her gigs, she had Mink there, her trusty cohort, on guitar.

"Is 'Mink' his real name?" I once asked, bemused that such a great guitarist should be identified with a small, furry animal.

Ruby snickered. "No, of course not. But that's what everybody calls him. He even has it on his driver's license."

How uncanny it was just to watch him warm up, producing a hair-raising array of wails, shrieks, and moans on his instrument, then turning methodically to adjust the knobs on his assortment of black boxes, as if such otherworldly sonorities were just business as usual.

Mink had a pixie-like appearance, short and thin, his shaggy dark hair surrounding a boyish face with a pug nose that twisted up slightly to one side and intelligent gray-blue eyes.

His walk, basically a swagger, had an easy grace to it, like that of a dancer.

His clothes, though less flamboyant than his playing, were still distinctive: tight-fitting jeans or black leather pants, contrasted with overly-layered, loose-fitting tops. He and Ruby were both fond of wearing Indian dress scarfs, wrapped loosely about the neck. He shunned bright colors, except for the occasional red. In general, Mink's clothes gave him the appearance of a wanderer.

"Gonna sing it 'cause I can..."

His voice, somewhat high for a man, could sound rough and virile when he shouted, or hypnotically sensuous when he approached a whisper. Sweating under the hot lights, he drew me in with every breath. He drew in everyone in the room. But everyone else could break the spell once the gig was over. I never could, nor did I want to.

* * *

I soon learned that Mink worked with a variety of bands besides Ruby's. Though hers remained by far my favorite, I tried to catch him anywhere he played, and became quite a student of his unique style.

He would do something in performance that I had never seen anyone else do: during his less-prominent parts, he would wander about the band, visiting each musician, and reacting with genuine delight to whatever that person happened to be playing at the moment. Mink would feed off their parts, developing incidental musical dialogues that were always more intriguing than whatever was going on centerstage.

It didn't matter what band he played in, whether he was in the spotlight or off in a corner somewhere. He played every note as if it were the most meaningful sound ever. Eyes closed, his face placid as a sleeping baby's, he would embroider the music, introducing sudden patches of brilliant color; he would tease and tantalize, hinting at a better place, a truer place, and for a short time, just the length of a guitar solo or an underlying riff, if we followed him, we were there.

At the same time I was terrified of him. Although I would always seek the seat closest to him, or the closest spot on the dance floor that I could get, during breaks I would retreat to the farthest corner of the club to hide from him. I half feared that close proximity to his radiance would incinerate me.

On one occasion it happened that a chamber music group in which I played the harp was to perform in the basement of the Music Gallery on the same day that the Blipskers, a children's group Mink played in with Toronto poet Eddie Noel, had a concert upstairs. During the break between our rehearsal and the concert, I heard muffled rock music coming from the main hall. I didn't dare go in – it was a children's concert, so why would I be there unless I were a stalker? But I sat pressed against the wall, drinking in whatever of their music I could imbibe that way.

* * *

Once at Grossman's, I happened to overhear this fragment of a conversation:

"Have you ever seen Ruby's boyfriend play?"

"Who's her boyfriend?"

"His name is Mink Lasher – he's an amazing guitarist."

I was stunned. Mink was Ruby's boyfriend? They behaved so casually, so freely with each other, like the best of friends rather than a couple. My own parents had such a tense, angry relationship, it was hard to believe that a man and woman could relate this way. I could only marvel at the romantic vision of these two bohemians living together, wild and free, in complete dedication to each other and to their art.

Once I knew of their romance, it puzzled me that I could have missed it before. It was positively magical how the two of them communicated onstage without words, connected through the music in such a profound way.

I pictured them as wild, exotic animals: dolphins, eagles, or perhaps gazelles. One was never far from the other in my mind, where together they would leap out of imaginary waters, soar through imaginary skies, or bound across endless expanses of a rapture I could hardly grasp.

Mink and Ruby seemed somehow removed from the usual progression of time, for I simply couldn't guess their age. They had the vivaciousness of youth, but their eyes often looked haggard and their skin showed many lines. Mink, in particular, had heavy bags under his eyes. I had no idea what could have caused this effect, although it intrigued me. As far as I was concerned, Mink and Ruby were simply unique, ethereal entities who inhabited a different plane of existence.

Their music sizzled. It burned. No stuffy concert hall housed them; they could take the most decrepid old tavern and turn it into a sacred palace of enchantment. I had never before known such transformative powers in art. They wrote their own songs, they improvised, creating new music right there on the spot. As a classically-trained musician, unable to play a single note not written down, I found this process utterly fascinating.

It didn't even strike me as strange that, except for our brief exchange at the Serpent's Plume, Mink never spoke to me throughout all of my doggedly following him from gig to gig. Why would he? After all, he dwelled in a separate universe from me. Once he sat down across from me at one of the long Grossman's tables and spoke with a gray-haired man in a fedora. "I still owe you that dough," Mink was saying, and I was surprised at how soft-spoken he was, compared to the onstage persona with which I was familiar. On another occasion, when I was sitting at a smaller table, he actually sat down beside me as his friends occupied the other chairs. "Could we get more space here?" he asked, which I understood as a hint for me to move but which I deliberately ignored, loath to give up this rare chance to sit with him.

These people were geniuses, truly inspired, extraordinary beings. Their poverty and the shabbiness of their surroundings only contributed to their glamor, as far as I was concerned. They were martyrs for their art. They were intellectual without being academic or stuffy. They were regal and austere, yet on fire with passion for what they did.

Meanwhile, the outside world, the world in which I spent most of my time, neither knew nor cared about them, didn't value their art, and had no way to comprehend their vision.

* * *

There were rituals I did to keep up with "my group." Sometimes they worked, but more often they simply left me frustrated and empty-handed. *NOW Magazine,* "The Streets of Ontario" on CFNY, the T.V. station MuchMusic, "The City Scene" on City-TV, concert advertisements in subways, the entertainment sections of the various newspapers,

Canadian Musician, *Canadian Composer*, *Rock Express*...I put my feelers into every media avenue I could think of. The fact that there was so little coverage of their activities made it that much more critical that I check every possible source.

Putting up posters was one of my most sacred rituals. I always made far too many copies: two or three hundred...I meant to put up all of them, but rarely succeeded. Out there with my posters and my masking tape, in all kinds of weather, I strove to carry out my mission.

I was always terrified of police cars. What would happen to me if I were caught? Would I be deported? That was the worst thing that I could imagine.

Eventually I developed a braver attitude towards the police: if I could see them, that meant that I knew where they were, so they couldn't sneak up on me. Each time I told myself that I liked "spotted" police cars; they were my friends. And if, with no police in sight, I still hesitated in fear, I would taunt myself: Are you waiting for the police?

Thursday was the day that *NOW Magazine* came out. I would walk blocks out of my way in search of a copy, despairing if it hit the streets late. It was a free weekly, printing the latest in city news and entertainment, presenting itself as a progressive, alternative publication, up with all the hippest, funkiest, kinkiest forms of culture.

The weekly *NOW* had an extensive section on music, reporting on the local personalities of the "indie" scene – independent musicians who had not yet been signed to a major record label. This magazine served as my main link to the vibrantly engaging artists who had become the center of my life.

* * *

It was a bit surreal being an American, or a "Yank," living in Canada. The language was the same; the cars drove on the same side of the street; clothes, hairstyles, food, and customs were generally the same. Still, there were political and cultural figures that had become household names here, and yet I knew nothing about them. Reading the newspaper often proved a baffling experience, since I was unacquainted with so many of the references and issues. The same did not hold true in the reverse sense – the Canadians I encountered all knew much more about American public figures than I did.

Poring through old copies of *Canadian Composer* and *Rock Express* in the Edward Johnson Building music library, once I became aware of this curious link with freedom up on the third floor, I learned of a whole new array of pop legends on the Canadian scene with whom Mink had played: Saga, Triumph, Neil Chapman, Rik Emmett, Dan Hill...

This information frustrated me as much as it impressed me. It seemed that my group had the Midas touch – everyone they worked with became famous, but not them. Was it their curse to be permanent denizens of the under-lit haunts of Toronto's club district?

Queen Street – that's where most of the nightclubs were: the Horseshoe, the Bamboo, the Cameron, the Rivoli...interspersed with *haute couture* clothing stores, specialty book shops, galleries, music stores, funky restaurants and cafes, frequented by herds of bohemians clad in black. Posters on telephone poles, lampposts, and the sides of buildings announced "upcoming" gigs, many of which were months past.

Ruby and I once arranged to meet at the vegetarian Earthtones Cafe, on Queen West across from the Bamboo. She had a lot of errands to do downtown that day; I had no business in that area, but was only too happy to make the journey. It was so strange to be seeing Ruby in the afternoon, I couldn't help wondering if her body would withstand contact with daylight.

I got there half an hour early and grabbed a New Age monthly and a window seat. The paper lay spread across the table, but I only made a pretense of reading it. My real attention was entirely focused out the window and at the door. Each time someone would enter, I started to readiness in almost military fashion.

At last the door opened and a frail-looking creature came into the shadows of the entranceway who could have been an old woman were it not for the smooth, ash-blond hair that fell down her back. A gray woolen jacket hung loosely about her delicate frame. From under a black beret her eyes caught mine and lit up, and I recognized that it was indeed Ruby.

"Hi there, Iris!" She took a moment to catch her breath. "I've been dragging around these stupid bags all morning – here, let me come over and set them down."

I jumped to my feet and hastily moved the paper out of the way. Her load, a mix of packages and bottles, looked more cumbersome than heavy. "What are those?" I asked.

Her breathing nearly back to normal, she removed her jacket. "Oh, just a bottle of patchouli – that's the perfume I wear, and...some herbal remedies I like to take. I get really excruciating menstrual cramps, and these are the only things that have ever helped me."

I had heard her complain before about inner pains. The strange workings of her body and her long-suffering endurance only added to her mystique. "I'm sorry. Are you in pain now?"

"No, no," she assured me. "My period isn't until next week." Relieved of her burden, she straightened up majestically and then looked over at the menu, which was written in colored chalk on a large blackboard. "Let's see, what do they have here?"

We walked together to the serving counter. Concoctions of bulgur, tofu and alfalfa sprouts were illuminated beneath the glass. "Do you have any desserts?" Ruby asked the woman behind the cash register, who gestured in the appropriate direction with a bland smile. "I have this terrible weakness for cakes and sweets," Ruby muttered, almost apologetically.

"You don't look it," I observed.

"That's not because of the way I eat!" she laughed. "I have this insanely high metabolism that keeps me skinny no matter what I put in my mouth. It used to be different, though. I was a fat kid."

I found this hard to believe.

Once Ruby had decided on a carrot cake slice and I had chosen a cherry bran muffin, we paid and brought our plates back to the table near the window, where sunbeams mingled with the artificial light of the cafe.

Ruby slumped back in her seat and sighed heavily. "I went to see this astrologer. I wanted to get a chart made up for Mink for his birthday – it's this Saturday. But we don't know what time he was born, so I couldn't get it done. I'll have to think of what else to get him instead." She looked so forlorn, weighed down by this comical problem, that I pitied her and at the same time found myself fascinated. No one in my family believed in astrology, and their skeptical attitude had always seemed sensible to me. Now it just seemed stifling. Dancing stars and swirling patterns of destiny surrounded Mink's birthday in my mind.

"I'm sure he'll like whatever you get him," I offered, trying to be helpful.

"Thanks." She laughed weakly, and her gaze drifted off into space. "Poor Mink! He's had it so rough, with Laird getting sick and the Sandalmen having to quit, and then them getting ripped off by Tiptoe Through, that pathetic excuse for a record label. It's been a really bad year for him...I hope he gets everything he wants."

I wanted to ask her more about all of this, but silence felt like the only appropriate response. We picked at our snacks, crumbs falling all over the plates.

Suddenly Ruby's face lit up. "My mother's housekeeper used to sing this song to me as a lullaby." I could barely hear the piped-in music, the voices around us were so loud, but Ruby murmured the words quietly: "*This little light of mine, I'm gonna let it shine.*" She smiled. "That's how I started singing, I just sang along with her." Ruby looked like a little girl all of a sudden, beaming in a childlike way.

* * *

Electric guitars had always scared me before, with their weird shrieks and howls, like cats fighting at night. Strange that Mink, the wielder of such an eerie instrument, should bring me such comfort. Always I would enter the clubs sheepishly, intimidated by the crowds. As soon as I caught sight of him, though, a rush of warmth would sweep through me, and I was at ease.

The music was always quite loud. I had learned from experience to bring earplugs with me if I didn't want my ears to ring with soreness for a day or two afterwards. It was loud even with earplugs, but having taken this slight precaution I felt justified in risking hearing loss, for this was where I needed to be.

* * *

Fleeing the listening lab one evening as my classmates continued to toil, I half-jogged, half-walked to Lee's Palace, a club about two miles west on Bloor Street. Colorful cartoon characters adorned the painted brick front. When I entered, I saw that the cartoon motif was continued inside.

There was a smattering of people. At a table near mine a woman tried, with increasing agitation, to get rid of a man who wanted to sit down next to her. Huddled within myself, I avoided getting involved. Soon another woman, no bigger than I, came by and fended him off. After the man slithered away, she pulled up a chair and the two women struck up a conversation.

By the time the band took the stage, more people had drifted in, and with most of them clustered towards the front, the main floor had the appearance of being half full.

It was Eddie Noel and the Lipkids that night. Eddie Noel, a pony-tailed local poet with a reputation for irreverence and often obscenity, fronted a five-piece outfit for which he wrote the lyrics and Mink, besides being guitarist, helped compose the music.

I had seen them a few times before and was able, by now, to sing along with most of the choruses.

During "Pistol Pop," one of the songs I knew well, Eddie stepped aside for what could have been a good twenty minutes while Mink embarked upon a guitar solo unlike any I had ever seen him do. Taking the front of the stage, he stared off into some other world as his notes grew longer and dreamier, having less and less to do with the song. His notes seemed to pose a question, which he asked again several times, each time the tone getting harsher and more piercing until the desperation was almost unbearable.

Then, as if a floodgate somewhere had burst, a torrent of music poured from his fingers, which struggled to keep up with the overwhelming current. It thrilled me to watch; I had the feeling that I was witnessing some sort of phenomenon that hadn't yet been documented.

Then, just as suddenly, the torrent subsided. But there was no relief; the question had never been answered, and all that was left was the quiet of devastation and of unquenchable longing.

The audience clapped and whistled. I put my hands together limply, rather shaken as Eddie came back to finish the song.

It was the last number of the evening. The band walked off, amidst applause and cheers. People started banging their beer bottles on the tables in unison. I picked up the ashtray in front of me and joined in.

Eventually Eddie Noel came back onstage. "Would you like a drummer?"

The audience cheered; the drummer returned to his place.

"Bring out the guitar player!" someone yelled nearby.

Eddie grinned. "Would you like a bass player?"

The fellow re-entered. And so it went until everyone but Mink had resumed his position.

"Well, that's everyone, isn't it?" Eddie asked. "Everyone I care about, anyway."

"What about the guitar player?" the man at the next table shouted at the top of his lungs.

"Well, okay, I guess we could have a guitar player."

"He's a real Pete Townsend!" It pleased me that this guy, whoever he was, recognized Mink's greatness, but he wasn't quite right. Mink was nothing like Pete Townsend. Mink was an original.

* * *

I had never been much of a drinker. Although I could tolerate beer, which my father had let me sip as a child so that I would fit in with the drinking crowd when I got older, I never bought it or ordered it on my own, imbibing only on those rare occasions when it was offered to me.

However, after I learned from Ruby that club owners preferred bands that kept things flowing at the bar, I made it a point to order as many expensive drinks as I could handle – two or three, depending on the strength. A couple of friends of mine, Peg and Pamela, had already introduced me to fuzzy navels, and I had grown fond of their tangy flavor.

From a restaurant's paper placemat that listed and described various cocktails, I discovered two more that would appeal to my sweet tooth: the Singapore sling and the grasshopper. It was the grasshopper that became my staple. I would order it anywhere I could, resorting to the others only at bars unequipped to serve the luscious mixture of creme de menthe, creme de cacao, and milk.

The waitstaff at Grossman's knew me on sight. All I had to do was sit down, and it would be a matter of minutes before a grasshopper would appear in a long-stemmed cocktail glass in front of me, cold and green, lumpy with crushed ice.

Dear old Grossman's, crawling with the drunkest of drunks, the air choking with cigarette smoke, aged photos pealing off the walls...I loved it. It was here that, in spite of ever-failing monitors and microphones, Mink would put on his best show.

"Three Amstels for the band..." He kissed the chubby waitress when she brought over a tray of beers.

An area in front, separated from the tables by speakers and minimal space for dancing, constituted what would have been a stage had it been raised. This closeness made for an almost electric connection between musicians and the audience.

So it was one evening when, during a performance of his song "Chemicals," Mink took his microphone into the audience. "You, sir," he said to a young, bearded man. "What's your favorite chemical?"

"Uh...P.C.B.'s."

"We've got a P.C.B. man here!" Mink wandered across the room. "How about you, ma'am? What chemical turns you on?"

"Dioxin!" the gray-haired woman, a regular, shouted with spirit.

"Dioxin!" He kissed her cheek. "Excellent choice!"

A young blonde rose from her chair.

"Hey, where are you going? You can't leave!" Mink exclaimed with mock alarm.

The woman laughed. "I'm just going to the bathroom!"

"Oh, you're gonna go pee?" The audience howled. "Never ask a lady where she's going!" Then he stepped back from the microphone and shut his eyes, his fingers resuming the groove. Once again he was inside the song.

CHAPTER 3

I became convinced that everything I was being taught at the Faculty of Music was fraudulent. Through my group I had experienced true music, and nothing that occurred in the Edward Johnson Building approached that.

Still, I had to stay in school and pass my courses, otherwise I would lose my student visa and my chance to live in Canada. So I plugged away within a system that was counterfeit, as far as I was concerned.

One Tuesday evening, as the hours dragged on in the practice room, I turned on my Walkman and happened to hear an ad for the radio show *Later, Man!* which that week was to feature a live interview with members of the Sandalmen.

My heart leapt. The Sandalmen...Laird...I ached to hear his voice, unbounded by the record grooves. Surely this was a sign: my group was at last rising from the ashes.

That Friday night, I tuned in a half hour early, as if that would ensure my readiness for the show. The horrid little room around me vanished as I focused on what came to me though my earphones.

Danny Hawks, the third founding member of the Sandalmen, was in the Toronto studio with the host; while all the way from Glasgow, Laird's smooth voice was beamed over, only slightly marred by static.

Mink wasn't present.

"Good evening to you both."

"Good evening."

"Good evening."

Was it really happening? I struggled to stay calm.

"So," the host continued, "I understand you guys have had some difficulties lately..."

"You could say that," Danny answered, his high voice sounding surprisingly chipper.

Laird's throaty chuckle burst in as if something highly amusing had been said. "We've faced a few hurdles, yes."

But as the interview went on, my glee turned into anger. The host's questions to Laird, all regarding his health, were awkward and rudely intrusive. Only Danny got to speak about the band and about musical ideas; Laird was treated as a medical case.

If the bandmates were angry, though, neither revealed it. Laird did his best to answer all the embarrassingly personal questions, offering: "I think I've been rather fortunate. There are other people who have much more serious problems, who haven't been as lucky as I was."

Danny, asked to describe the dynamics of the band, praised his colleagues: "Well, Mink is an excellent lead guitarist, Laird plays great acoustic, and I play acoustic as well... we all share in writing the music, so it has an odd sort of balance to it."

I pictured Laird, Mink, and Danny together, a pantheon of talent, inspiring each other in the harmony of creation. But I cringed as the interview shifted, once again, to the subject of Laird's dialysis treatments, three times a week, the nurses were very kind, yes...

Then the show was over.

"Thank you for having us!" Danny chimed.

"Yes, thanks Steve," Laird added in his much deeper voice. "It's been great."

The *Later, Man!* theme music returned, and once again I was alone in a room in the basement.

* * *

That interview, humiliating as it was, made me optimistic that I might start to hear more about the Sandalmen, and maybe about Ruby and Mink. But I didn't. Even an article in *T.O. Magazine* that celebrated ten years of outstanding Toronto bands contained no mention of anyone connected with my group.

During theory class, as the teaching assistant droned on, I pretended to take notes but instead jotted down a rough draft of a letter to the editor.

How can you have an article about "Ten Years of Toronto Bands" without including the Sandalmen? Then I went on to plug Mink: *Canada's finest guitarist;* and Ruby: *a brilliant singer/songwriter and a captivating performer.* I ended with: *I hope to see a much more comprehensive review of Toronto's music scene in your publication before another decade goes by!*

I got a failing grade on my next theory quiz, but my letter did make it into the glossy pages of *T.O. Magazine.*

It was almost beyond belief. For *T.O. Magazine* could be found at newsstands everywhere – not only in the largest bookstores, but also in the tiny shops in subway stations. I would take great pleasure in just passing by as many magazine racks as I could find, just to catch sight of the edition, bearing a shiny black car and a blonde model on its cover, that contained my letter.

Ruby and her band had a gig at the Horseshoe that Thursday night. "We loved your letter! It was quite humorous," she told me when I called about getting my name put on the guest list. Embarrassed and overjoyed, I felt surrounded by a bubble of cosmic goodwill as I walked the two-or-so miles to the club.

It tickled me when, during the course of the gig, my letter became the topic of stage banter. Mink actually grinned at me when he referred to Ruby as "one of Toronto's hidden treasures and a truly brilliant singer."

"'Singer-slash-songwriter,'" Ruby corrected him, quoting my letter in jest.

Excited shivers went through me. I looked down and took convulsive sips of my fuzzy navel.

But the rest of the concert didn't go very well. There were problems with the new arrangements of a couple of their songs. Although it all sounded exquisite to me, Ruby's grimaces as well as the ominously muted band conferences between songs suggested that a lot had gone wrong. At the end of the last set, hailed by a smattering of applause, Ruby withdrew behind a curtain.

I waited at my table, hoping that she would come out and talk to me, or at least I could say goodbye to her. The club emptied around me. Eventually I decided I might as well go. I glumly rose to my feet and gathered up my book, purse, and jacket, all in slow motion, in case she should come out again after all. I was beginning to slide my chair in when someone called out: "Iris!"

Could it be? I turned around, and there was Mink, coming towards me, his hand outstretched. I hesitantly gave him my own limp hand and he shook it. "Thanks for that letter!"

"Y-you guys were great tonight," I stammered.

He released my hand and rubbed his stubbly cheek. "Ruby would really like to hear that right now."

How unreal it seemed, that Mink Lasher himself should be standing here, chatting with me like an ordinary person. "So," I ventured to ask, "is playing here different from playing at Grossman's?"

"Totally different." Mink sat down in the chair in front of me; awestruck, I continued to stand. "The overall balance, the way you can hear yourself onstage...It's totally different." He stood up again. "I think Ruby would really like to hear you say that. Why don't you go over and tell her? Do you know where she is?"

"N-no."

He put his right arm around my shoulders and, with his left hand, pointed to a door that opened onto the stage. "See that room? Ruby's in there. She would really like to hear that." He squeezed my shoulder once and then let me go.

Like someone hypnotized, I walked towards the door and went inside.

Ruby was sitting in a wooden chair in a corner of the room. Delilah Zed, a raven-haired Wicca priestess who sometimes sang background vocals with her at Grossman's and who always dressed like a witch, was standing next to her. Ruby looked up as I entered and smiled wanly at me.

"You were wonderful," I said.

Ruby only shook her head. "It's always such a nightmare for me. I hated being out there. I hated every minute of it..."

Mink had talked to me. He had come over and...

"It's because my mother was always tearing me down," Ruby was saying. "She would sometimes lock me in the closet, she was so crazy. My father was a sweet guy, but my mother was such a neurotic. And it's made me neurotic, too. I'm always negative about things. In fact, Mink almost left me because I was so negative. And I know it must be really hard for him, having to put up with me being like this..." Shrouded in her black shawl like a widow, she looked so sad, so forlorn.

"I wish she were here so I could beat her up!" Delilah said, simulating a karate kick.

Ruby laughed feebly.

"The music was great," I said. My hand had started shaking in giant spasms. I hoped neither of them would notice.

* * *

It seemed to me that Mink was a real celebrity. *NOW* regularly reported his myriad gigs, speaking of him in familiar terms, as if he were everyone's friend. At the clubs, he would engage the audience while onstage, and offstage, he was nearly always surrounded by a circle of his buddies. Everyone knew Mink Lasher.

Actually, no one knew Mink Lasher. The Canadian publications for sale on the magazine racks, even those focusing on musicians, contained scarcely a mention of him. Not one of the students I talked to had ever heard of him, though some knew of the Sandalmen. Mink played in the seediest bars, and could draw a crowd only at Grossman's, where the regulars would deliver awed though slurred tributes to him over their beers.

A month later he had a stint at Lee's Palace, with Eddie Noel again.

I sat there alone, reading a book, hoping Mink would come over to my table. Of course, I avoided looking at him – after all, I didn't want him to think I was desperate.

But he never did come by. He spent the breaks conversing sullenly with the guys in the band, or alone at the bar. During the course of the evening he didn't say a word to me or acknowledge my presence in any way. But I was used to that. Perhaps, except for very rare, special occasions, this was the way it was to be.

* * *

Peg and Pamela, my lesbian friends down the block, had introduced me to the music of Denise d'Angereuse, the infamous bisexual rock diva from Montreal. To all of our delight, it turned out that she was to perform at the Diamond Club, with Mink in her band.

I might have been able to get us onto the guest list, but was far too shy to ask this favor about such a major concert. So, having bought our pricey tickets like everybody else, we made it down to the posh venue and pushed our way through packed bodies towards the stage.

The atmosphere was hot with anticipation, but while everyone around me eagerly awaited Denise d'Angereuse, I yearned for Mink.

At last the band made their entrance, coming down a spiral staircase amidst a cloud of dry ice fumes. Denise's exaggerated make-up, excessive curls, and black leather outfit set the tone. Mink, too, wore tight black leather pants, accentuating his slender physique. Meanwhile, a gigantic T.V. screen overhead magnified everything onstage and made it visible to those in back.

Mink dove into the hard rock grooves with abandon, not with macho posturing but in his facile, impish way. At one point he even simulated oral sex with Denise during a particularly sensuous guitar solo, but it was done with such grace and artistry that nothing about it seemed crude. Throughout the concert he and Claude, the other guitarist, would trade off soloing, but Claude could barely keep up with Mink's virtuosity and vigor. Still, Mink would raise his bottle of Amstel in salute, grinning encouragingly at his counterpart.

I loved seeing Mink's blissful face when it appeared on the giant screen, and the close-up shots of his hands on the guitar.

After the show, our ears ringing, the three of us emerged from the club into the bracingly chilly night air. Peg and Pamela raved about Denise d'Angereuse while I smiled to myself, still seeing Mink's enormous visage, no larger than life to me.

* * *

The reviews were awful. Mink Lasher had "grandstanded," had "marred the event with his buffoonery and made a travesty out of everything..." One critic in *Music Express* had panned Denise d'Angereuse but praised the band, citing Mink and his "rambunctious heavy metal stunts;" that critic was the exception.

I sat at a long, wooden table in Grossman's, listening in on the men's conversation around me and ingesting smoke.

"Did you see the picture in *The Sun*? The one with him standing right in front of Denise d'Angereuse?"

"Poor Mink!"

"It's because he has so much soul."

Mink, fortunately, was in another part of the room, discussing something with the bass player.

The barbs against Mink felt like barbs against me, and I drank down my grasshopper much too quickly.

* * *

The first snowflakes fell, and I dreaded another Toronto winter. Meanwhile, though, the city decked itself out in colored lights and glitter with the approach of Christmas.

Skimming through the co-op's daily edition of *The Globe and Mail* one evening I noticed a holiday event going on at Harbourfront called "Festive Trees." It involved various local celebrities and groups decorating Christmas trees. People visiting the exhibit could "vote" for their favorite tree by contributing money in its designated box, with all proceeds going to UNICEF. Among the featured participants were the Sandalmen.

I had never been to Harbourfront before, though I had often heard about its activities and shops and been tempted to explore. The article listed a phone number which I called to get directions since I had no idea how to get there.

And so it happened that, one frightfully gusty day, I found myself shivering outside Union Station, awaiting the arrival of a special shuttle bus, bearing a giant golden wind-up key on top. When at last it came and I stepped inside, I was transported south to an airy complex of buildings overlooking Lake Ontario.

In spite of the bitter cold, I felt exhilarated by the vista of water spreading to the horizon. Nearer by, people scurried about to do their

Christmas shopping or to take their children to the various holiday entertainments Harbourfront had to offer.

Walking into what looked like the main building, I found a map that directed me to the area of the Festive Trees. I had to brave the elements again as I crossed the plaza to get to the right location; once inside, though, the display was easy to find.

I meandered through long rows of glistening trees. Some had humorous decorations such as pop cans or old shoes or toy animals. Others were ornamented in traditional ways. A hand-printed sign at the base of each tree gave the name of the entity who had decorated it.

I started to feel vaguely homesick, looking at all these symbols of family togetherness here in these cold, breezy halls.

The other parts of Harbourfront had been far more crowded. Here I was practically alone, except for one mother and young daughter much further down the aisle. Their high voices echoed unintelligibly to me.

Then I saw it. From a cardboard sign, the name "Sandalmen" blazed in blue-and-gold letters.

The tree was covered with old 45 rpm records, alternated with candy canes and gingerbread men. In front stood a wooden box with a slot near the top in which coins could be inserted.

I glanced around. Seeing no one, I took out my overstuffed wallet. Somehow I managed to shove into the little slot a total of two hundred fifty-three dollars and sixty-eight cents, in small bills and whatever change I had.

* * *

A couple of weeks after winter vacation, Ruby's band gigged again at Grossman's. Having braved the nippy air all afternoon and into the evening to put up band posters I had made, I finally rewarded myself by entering the smoky warmth of the club.

It was fairly crowded, and the best seat I could find was at the central table, much farther away from the stage area than I would have liked to be. I scooted the chair out and, hanging my coat and scarf on its back, prepared to sit down.

"Hi, Iris!" Mink rubbed my back vigorously as he passed behind me. The rub metamorphosed into a tender stroke.

A warm glow spread through me. My back tingled as I took my seat.

The band went on before long, featuring a guest drummer who had apparently played with Kim Mitchell. I enjoyed the set, but when it ended I realized with guilt that I had barely paid attention.

During the break I took my obligatory trip to the graffiti-covered women's room and hid there for a while. Then I started to pick my way back through the crammed aisles in the direction of my seat.

Mink appeared in front of me. "Let me buy you a beer," he said.

I stood there stunned, daring to look only at his black sweatshirt, at my eye level.

"What kind?" he asked.

"You like Amstel," I noted with a silly laugh.

"I like Amstel," he repeated, as if baffled that I would know this. "Tonight I'm drinking this stuff..." and he held up a bottle of Moosehead, "but I'll buy you an Amstel." He went to the bar and, after joking with the waitress, ordered me a beer while I stood there, positively shaking from his proximity.

He returned and handed me the bottle. "That was pretty funny about Harbourfront."

"Cute tree!" I remarked.

"Cute tree," he said, again repeating my words, but this time with a tongue-in-cheek grin. Then he went on in a hurried stream about their photo session at the Festive Tree event, and all the gifts they had received from UNICEF: posters, cards, and a calendar. "We'll give them all to you, of course," he said, tapping my shoulder.

That was the last I ever heard about those gifts, but that night at Grossman's was gift enough for me.

* * *

Thereafter, I could count on hearing Mink call out, "Hi, Iris!" from across the room whenever he saw me enter, a merry glint in his eye. I think it amused him that I was so shy. Sometimes he would surprise me with a bear hug, or a sudden kiss on the cheek. I loved the sensation of his stubble brushing against my skin, and the scent of beer on his breath. My father had kissed me like that, and just as it had then it made me feel warm and protected.

And Mink had a unique ability to clear my mind. Like Moses parting the Red Sea, he could scatter my worries with one smile, or one note on his guitar.

The Grossman's regulars were entranced with him, too.

"He's a true artist! I've seen him play with all kinds of bands, and with each band he does whatever is needed. It's not always 'chung, chung.' Whatever is needed. That's the mark of a true artist."

"He plays that guitar like he was making love to a woman."

"Last week he was playing at this place on Bathurst, and he just went at it until four in the morning. He never stops!"

Hearing those inebriated gentlemen speak of Mink in this way helped give me the courage of my convictions.

"He should be famous," I once said to Devin, a ruddy-faced friend of theirs to whom Ruby had introduced me. "He's too good just to be playing here."

"Hey," Devin replied with a shrug, "I have fun coming here to listen to him. If he just plays here, it's fine with me."

I smiled, but inwardly seethed at his indifference to the plight of his friend.

Mink's versatility as a musician mirrored his versatility as a man. It amazed me that he seemed able to relate so comfortably to so many types of people. As someone who found most people extremely difficult, I was fascinated by this. He could communicate on an artistic level with the musicians in the bands he played in. He could be a loud, boisterous drinking buddy to the guys at the bar, becoming tough and threatening as necessary, when anyone got out of hand. He could be gentle and "yin-like," as Ruby put it, when speaking with women, caring about their personal issues. Which of these was the true Mink? It was a question I loved to ponder.

"Hey, not bad for a white guy!" a burly, bearded man exclaimed, slapping Mink on the back after a particularly fiery set. Mink, laughing, turned and embraced him like a brother.

* * *

Once Mink even made the cover of *NOW Magazine,* standing beside a pop singer named Trudy Artman.

When I called immediately after seeing it, Ruby answered. "Hi, Iris! I'm stirring a big pot of spaghetti right now, and it's bubbling over!"

Breathless with praises, I bubbled over as well, adding, "except that he's with the wrong woman!"

Ruby laughed. "No, she's famous. It's good. Good for Mink."

Ruby and Mink. They accepted me in my lonely, waif-like state – they were parents and friends to me, they were wild birds who carried me on their wings to freedom.

I didn't know exactly what I was to them – some sort of overgrown child, perhaps. Still, I assumed that the relationship I had with my group was normal, was a common sort of thing that everyone experienced; and that the reason I hadn't heard of anything like it before was that I was young and naive. Someday I would have to ask someone about it, and surely then I would learn its proper name.

CHAPTER 4

The new school year brought me a room of my own, finally, in a house on Huron Street, part of the same co-op system. No longer forced to languish in the Edward Johnson Building dungeon, I spent most of my time alone in my room, practicing with the T.V. on in the background – luxury of luxuries! – or reading, or decorating my walls with little cut-out articles pertaining in some way to my group.

This house had its own kitchen and no meal plan, meaning that I could buy my own food, which I did mostly at Noah's, a nearby health food store on Bloor Street. I still lived mainly on cereal and sandwiches, but they were concocted from organically-grown ingredients of my choosing. Eating alone in my room, I barely needed to speak to my housemates at all. That suited me just fine.

My bed never got made; it was all I could do to keep the sheet on the mattress. Newspapers, magazines, and class assignments littered my floor. Sometimes a dish or cup from the previous night's dinner would still be there the next morning, but as long as it didn't smell, I didn't care. This was *my* room, and I could do what I wanted. Here I was free.

* * *

At the beginning of October, I saw advertised in *NOW* a gig by the Sunswayers, to take place at the Diamond. The Sunswayers, whom I had seen a few times before, were a reggae band becoming increasingly popular across Canada. Sometimes criticized for being too "soft," the band featured two frontmen: Jimbo Mackey, a white singer/saxophone player, and Burton Willis, a black singer/rhythm guitarist. These two wrote most of the band's material. They sang about peace and interracial harmony, but mostly about love. Their buoyant music got people dancing every time. And Mink had recently become their guitarist.

I hadn't seen or called either Ruby or Mink since my return from summer vacation. Although I missed them desperately, I feared that I had imposed myself on them too much before and that I ought to control myself better. So, instead of calling to get on the guest list, as I had often done in the past, I simply showed up at the club on Sherbourne Street.

Denise d'Angereuse's concert had seen the Diamond bursting with people, but tonight's event was more modestly attended. I couldn't find my ID at first, and panicked as I fumbled through the accumulated junk in my purse. But at last I found the card which was not a driver's licence, since I couldn't drive, but a photo ID nonetheless proving that I was old enough to enter.

I handed over my jacket and a few coins at the coat check counter and turned around.

There he was, right in front of me in the hallway. "Iris, you should have told me you were coming. I would have put your name on the guest list," Mink reproved me.

I felt embarrassed, having tried to avoid getting on his nerves and yet having done just that. I bit my lip. "Is Ruby coming?" I asked.

"No, she couldn't make it tonight. She got tied up doing other things." Mink kicked at the wall with the heel of his cowboy boot, and I noticed how surprisingly petite his feet were. "Well, I gotta go get set up," he said after a minute, and disappeared into the darkened interior of tho club.

Heart pounding, I scurried to the nearby washroom and leaned against the tiled wall to steady myself.

Though I would certainly have an abysmal harp lesson in the morning, it hadn't been a mistake for me to come. It never was.

As more people straggled into the club and I heard sounds of the band warming up, I ventured into the main room and drifted about near the stage until the show began.

As usual with the Sunswayers, Mink remained in the background most of the time, definitely a sideman, but the focus of all my attention. His little riffs, minimal as they were, seemed like a sly, running commentary on the main action, somehow mocking and enriching it at the same time.

Finally, he stepped forward to do a solo. Glistening with

perspiration, he shouted something in Jimbo's ear and the two of them laughed heartily; then he began.

Simple notes, nothing flashy at the start. He bent one of the notes in a way that sounded almost comical, and I was about to smile when it turned into the most gut-wrenching wail. That was just the beginning.

It horrified me, rather like watching someone turn inside out and reveal his internal organs: palpitating heart, blood-soaked liver and intestines...I felt somewhat guilty, as if by being there I were participating in some form of human sacrifice.

The solo drew to a close. Mink acknowledged the audience's applause and then withdrew into the background again, staring impassively before him as he resumed his sparse accompaniment.

I made it back to the co-op that night in a daze, not even bothering to brush my teeth or take off my clothes before going to bed.

And my prediction came true: my lesson the next day *was* abysmal.

* * *

Peg and Pamela agreed to come with me to one of Ruby's gigs. I had recommended that they stay till the end, since that was when the most intense jamming usually took place. I offered them earplugs, which they refused, and then complained about how loud it was; Pamela didn't like the smoke; they called Grossman's a "dive," ridiculed Ruby's clothes, and left after one set.

Of course, I stayed until the bitter, beautiful end.

"Interesting encore!" I exclaimed as Mink engulfed me in a bear hug.

"Wasn't it, though!" he laughed, releasing me.

It had been, too. Actually, the band had played two encores that night. The first, a raucous rendition of "These Boots Were Made for Walking" (one of the few cover tunes I had heard them do) had left the audience clamoring for yet another encore. Amidst the drunken shouts and the clanging of bottles and ashtrays on the tabletops, Mink alone had returned to the stage area. As he picked out a few seemingly aimless notes on the guitar, the noise subsided. The notes gradually became more sustained, but no more cohesive. Where was he going with this? I was accustomed to the misleadingly flippant beginnings of his solos, but this one continued in its haphazard fashion long after it should have taken flight. Still, the tones were gentle, almost constituting a strange lullaby. After several minutes of this, he stopped abruptly, bowed, and left the stage area.

"See," Mink now explained to me, "when we were playing, the energy kept getting higher and higher." He did an upwardly spiraling motion with his finger to show what he meant. "Where can you go from there? I just had to calm things down."

I smiled. "Well, you did!"

As Mink's attention got diverted by a denim-clad couple, I sought out Ruby. She was seated at a table by a window at the front of the club, slumped over in her chair. Hesitantly I approached her.

"Oh, hi, Iris." Her tired face brightened a bit. "Thanks for coming."

I drew closer. "That was wonderful!"

"Thanks, but..." She groaned. "My voice sounded terrible tonight! I think it's some of the crap I've been eating lately. It's catching up to me. And then the band was *way* too loud. I've tried to talk to them about turning it down, but...they just won't listen."

"Well, it sounded great to me!"

She grimaced and squeezed my arm. "You're sweet."

* * *

With Ruby and Mink, I often felt as if I were walking up a sand dune. Every time I seemed to be making progress in getting closer to them, my foothold would slip away. They would be warm, familiar, and confidential on one occasion, but then the next time I saw them they would be distant, or even ignore me altogether. This was true of them individually and as a pair. Their aloofness left me feeling broken, as if I were disintegrating. I had no explanation for their changeable manner, and was too timid to bring up the subject. So I just accepted it, with all the turmoil it caused me. The distance never lasted; warmth followed coolness; neither was a permanent condition.

* * *

The next time I called Ruby, she told me something she had forgotten to mention at her gig. The band was scheduled to record a few songs that might eventually go on an album. They had booked time in a studio for Friday night, and I was invited to come. After a muttered exchange with Mink that went on for a few minutes, she apologized and gave me the street number and directions.

So, as soon as I could possibly make it after my school orchestra concert that Friday, I hurried down to Phoebe, a tiny sidestreet off Spadina Avenue, just below Chinatown. The street itself was residential; I walked briskly past an elementary school and its empty playground. It was nearly pitch black. If I had been anyplace but Toronto, I would have felt afraid; but here in my city, on my streets, no harm could come to me.

Ruby had described the loading dock area of the building that contained the studio. A couple of blocks down Phoebe Street, I came upon a place that appeared to fit the description. It was at the base of what had probably been a factory once; now, it was merely one of those tall, forbidding industrial buildings that seemed to dominate the Spadina area.

I went inside. The warm, musty air stung my face, and only then did I realize how cold I had been. A naked lightbulb hung by a wire from the ceiling. The elevator claimed to be out-of-order, and I believed it. Off to the left, a rickety staircase led to the upper floors. Ruby had told me that the studio was on the second floor, so up I went.

Near the second-floor landing, a man snored loudly, sprawled out on the stairs. Holding my breath, I tiptoed past him to the landing. Around the corner I found a closed door bearing the correct number, 207 B, in tarnished brass, and I knocked.

There was music inside; faintly, I could make out bits of Ruby's song, "Together Time." I waited, and knocked again.

The man on the stairs continued to snore. I was getting rather apprehensive. The music must have been very loud inside, for no one seemed to hear my repeated knocking. Increasingly upset, I stood watching my boots drip tiny brown puddles onto the broken tiled floor, and I wondered what I was doing here.

Then the music stopped. I stood up and banged on the door as loudly as I could.

At last the door opened and a young blond man let me in. "I'm Doug," he said, shaking my hand. He led me into a room to the right, with enormous speakers stacked up in back and two large windows looking out over the blackened street.

Mink grinned and waved at me when I entered. He was sitting in a swivel chair in front of a large table. "Did you bring the beer?" he asked.

"No," I laughed.

He heaved a theatrical sigh. "Then what good are you?"

Doug gestured for me to sit down on the maroon vinyl couch at the back of the room. And that's when I saw that what appeared to be a table was actually a console full of dials. I had never been in a studio before.

"Is Iris here? Hi, Iris." Ruby's disembodied voice came from somewhere. I looked around and finally saw her right in front of me, wearing headphones, in a small, isolated booth behind a window.

"Hi, Ruby!"

"You were a little sharp that last time. Try it again." Mink slouched in his chair and folded his hands on his belly.

Ruby took a sip of water and then approached the microphone. "I'm ready."

Doug started the music – it was a passage in the middle of the song. Ruby entered, *"Dreams flow from my glass of wine..."* Then, abruptly, Doug stopped the music.

"How was that?" Ruby asked.

Mink took a deep breath and released it with a huff. "You're not quite getting it."

"Well, was it sharp again or what?"

"It was sharp, and it sounded...just try it again."

Ruby tore off her headphones and threw them down.

"What is she doing?" Mink grumbled.

I didn't understand what I had walked in on, but it was making me very tense. Ruby's singing had sounded fine to me.

After a couple of minutes, Ruby put on her headphones again and resumed her place in front of the microphone. "Is everyone ready?" she asked, although it sounded like an order.

Doug started up the music. *"Dreams flow from my glass of wine..."* The music stopped.

Mink buried his face in his hands.

"Would somebody please say something?" Ruby demanded.

Mink slowly dragged his hands down his face, stretching and distorting his features. "She's getting tired," he said, standing up. He walked over to the door of the booth and opened it. "It stinks in here!" he exclaimed. "Didn't you use deodorant?"

"Well, it's hot!"

"I'm kidding! I'm kidding!" Mink wrapped his arms around her and kissed the top of her head. Then the two of them spoke to each other alone, quietly, inside the booth.

Doug turned to me. "So, are you a musician, too?" he asked.

I talked to him about my harp playing and my classes, all the while staring through the booth window at a conversation I couldn't hear.

After several minutes Mink came out.

Ruby adjusted her headphones. "Ready," she said.

Doug started the music, taking it yet again from the keyboard intro to the third verse.

"Dreams flow from my glass..." She stopped. Her words came through clenched teeth: "My voice just isn't warmed up yet!"

"You should have been warming up during the day," Mink countered.

"Stop trying to make me feel guilty!" Ruby snapped back.

Mink pleadingly looked up to the heavens. "I'm not trying to...hey, if you feel guilty, it's not *my* fault!"

They started to do another take. Midway through, Ruby

growled, "Forget it. I need to take a break." The door of the booth opened and she came out, looking thoroughly worn and weary.

Mink got up and, putting his arm around her waist as he might have done with a cripple, helped her across the room to the chair where he had been sitting. It surprised me when he then scooped her up onto his lap. "Release it, let go, surrender," he murmured over and over, stroking her back.

Ruby shut her eyes as if contacting some inner point of strength; then she opened them again and stood up. "Well, let's go again," she said with renewed vigor.

Then began another grueling session. It perplexed me that, painful as the process obviously was, both Ruby and Mink seemed driven to work on endlessly, apparently losing all track of time or place. At one point Mink went into the booth with Ruby to coach her on her phrasing. *"Dreams flow from my glass of wine..."* Then Mink sang it, with looser vibrato, and Ruby tried again.

Glancing at the clock, I noticed that the green digits read one-thirty-six. Here, in this dingy, god-forsaken studio, these two were pushing themselves to the breaking point. But why? Outside the walls of this place, they didn't exist. What did it matter if what they did was perfect or mediocre, or if they gave up altogether?

I turned to Doug. "Are all your clients as ultra-perfectionistic as they are?" I asked.

He laughed and shook his head. "Nope! Definitely not!"

"Dreams flow..." As I watched them through the window, laboring together so earnestly over this one line, it occurred to me that they might both be insane.

CHAPTER 5

More and more I felt imprisoned. My harp teacher continued on her quest to take over my life, instructing me about what to wear for harp performances, how to style my hair...she even picked out glasses frames for me. Peg, whom she had met and deemed quite fashionable, was charged with the task of teaching me how to walk, so that I could make a grand entrance upon the stage.

The direction was to keep the upper body totally still, and not to bounce, as I was prone to do. I would pace back and forth across Peg and Pamela's living room, trying to glide...

I felt stiff, like a zombie. My feet hurt in the high-heeled shoes my teacher had told me to wear.

When Peg and Pamela nodded their approval, my agony was complete.

* * *

Ruby sported a handmade, beaded cross on a cord around her neck at the next Grossman's gig.

"Are you a Christian?" I asked, feeling vaguely alienated. I myself had grown up agnostic.

"No," she answered, "I don't think I would identify with most people who call themselves Christians. But I believe in Christ-consciousness." She sighed. "I can't stand it in here. I need to go outside and get some air." As an afterthought she added: "You can come, if you want."

I followed her out, happy to do so. We stood in the yellow glow of the Grossman's marquee. The night air that chilled me seemed to invigorate her. She inhaled deeply, her glossed lips spreading into a rapturous smile.

A police car sped by, and Ruby again appeared to notice me and her surroundings. She resumed the conversation. "Yes, Christians can be so narrow-minded, with all their little opinions. And I'm tired of opinions. I want enlightenment!" She tossed back her golden mane as if in defiance. I marveled at this woman, so beautiful and so free.

Then she told me about the meditation group she had begun to attend. "They have this guru that they worship, a guy from India." She emphasized the second syllable of "guru" as I had never heard the word pronounced before. "I'm not really into that whole 'guru thing,' but I like the meditation part. Actually, you might like it, too." She turned and looked at me. "I worry about you, Iris. Sometimes I think of you, and I feel that you're suffering."

This puzzled me, since I didn't consider myself to be suffering. Still, it touched me that she would express such concern.

So it was that, one Sunday afternoon, I found myself in a basement full of people sitting on mats chanting "Amuram-ham-madhuram-ham." Closing my eyes, I tried to focus my energy as they directed. But it was Ruby's presence rather than anything they said that "awakened my spiritual core," to use their terminology.

After the session, Ruby and I gathered up our coats. Reaching into her bag, she offered me a bottle of cranberry-kiwi nectar. "It's very good for cleansing the system," she told me.

"That was fun," I said, not sure how much of it I had understood but wanting to be interested in anything that interested her.

On the way to the streetcar stop, Ruby explained things further. "I think that relating to a spiritual leader is like being a tuning fork."

I found myself laughing, until she elaborated: "Some people resonate with one frequency, and some might respond to a different frequency. It doesn't mean that one is right and the others are wrong. Anyway, I like being with a group of people who are all mindful of a higher plane."

I knew exactly what she meant.

* * *

The bohemian tide had swept over me in my chaotic room. I would stay up sometimes past three in the morning, jotting down poetry fragments and ideas, scribbling out symbolic drawings, making lame attempts at playing by ear, and listening – at an acceptably quiet volume – to CFNY. The atmospheric music lifted me out of the white-walled confinement of my room into a realm of spaciousness and freedom.

David Sylvian, Bryan Ferry, Jane Siberry, Simple Minds, Kate Bush, Orchestral Maneuvers in the Dark...the hypnotic grooves, combined with the giddiness induced by sleep deprivation, took me into a trance-like state. This was *my* time.

* * *

Mink had put together a new band, called Loudest Rain, featuring himself as frontman. Accompanying him were players who had earned reputations in bands like the Pukka Orchestra and Parachute Club and on the jazz scene. Ruby and a throaty woman soul singer who had done commercials handled the background vocals.

The band premiered at the Silver Dollar, attracting a larger-than-usual crowd of fans of the respective musicians. Needless to say, the band, and particularly Mink, put on quite a dazzling show. And needless to say, there was no press coverage whatsoever.

I just could not accept that.

In the letter I sent to the editor of *NOW* I may have erred on the flowery side, employing such adjectives as "vertiginous" and "transcendent" to describe Mink's playing. But my letter did appear, slightly shortened, in *NOW*'s pages two weeks later.

As exciting as that was for me, I also felt acutely embarrassed. What would Mink think of me? My ever-present fear of being seen as a stalker, or at best a fawning sycophant, seized me to the point of hyperventilation each time I would try to look at my letter in print.

What was worse: Mink had a gig with the Sunswayers that very evening at the Bamboo, and I needed to call to remind him to put my name on the guest list.

It took me about an hour to summon up the courage. Several times I picked up the receiver and began to dial, only to hang up midway through. At last, though, I bit the bullet and finished dialing the call.

My heart pounded unbearably as the phone rang two, three times...would I get away with just leaving a message on their machine?

Someone picked up the phone. "Hallo." It was Mink's voice, so strong and forceful I felt myself shrinking away.

"Hi, this is Iris."

To my delight, Mink chuckled on the other end. "Hi."

"Just reminding you to put my name on the guest list."

He laughed. "Sure, after that write-up!"

"Well, see you tonight."

"See ya."

* * *

The Sunswayers took a break.

Fuzzy navel in hand, I stood near a painted brick column and nodded to the beat of the reggae background music, trying to appear perfectly at ease.

The club was nearly packed. If only Ruby's band or Loudest Rain could attract an audience like this! Maybe someday...

Someone squeezed my shoulders twice. "I don't know what made you do it, but I'm glad you did."

I turned around. "Well, someone had to!"

He stood there, beer in hand, in his Betty Boop t-shirt, still looking quite solemn. "It was a kind thing to do. A humane thing to do." He looked around. "Let's go upstairs."

We made our way through the crowd to the rear of the club. "How can you learn the music for all these different bands?" I shouted at his back.

He heard me. "I don't know," he laughed. "I don't understand it myself. It's an enigma!"

Cryptic Mink. His talents apparently astonished him as much as they astonished me, and he wasn't shy about admitting it. Yet it didn't sound conceited the way he said that. It simply confirmed what I already believed about him: that he was a mysterious being, in tune with forces much larger than himself. It intrigued me, fascinated me.

Mink pushed open a door behind the stage and we went through. A hallway stacked with cardboard boxes led to a stairway. "Oh, you're famous, by the way," he told me as we went up. "Everyone saw your letter."

On the second floor, a cluster of people had gathered in a shabby area with chairs and a refrigerator, which a paper sign on the door labeled the "Green Room." I recognized the bass and keyboard players of the Sunswayers; the others were strangers to me. Mink introduced me as "Iris, the famous letter-writer, and also," he added, grinning at me, "an internationally-renowned harpist." I could feel myself blushing, not so much because of his exaggerated compliment as from the thrill of being there as his honored guest.

A husky, gray-haired man gripped Mink by the shoulder and gave him a good-natured shake. "Admit it, Mink. You wrote that letter and you're just saying she did it."

"No," Mink chuckled, "it was all her." After mingling a bit, for he seemed to know everybody, he went to the refrigerator and, taking out a couple of beers, handed me one. "Cheers!" He clinked my beer can with his, then scrunched his face into a mock grimace. "I was hoping there'd be some weed up here, but there ain't! Let's go."

I followed him out into the hallway. "Oh, I wanted to ask you, did I get the name of the band right?"

"You got the name of the band exactly right. Everything was perfect." He stepped back and leaned against the wall, a faraway look coming over his eyes. "Did Ruby tell you how I came up with that name?"

"No, she didn't."

He took a sip of beer. "I had this dream: I was walking through an Aztec temple with a high priest and his followers. They were taking me to be...they needed me for some religious ritual. Anyway, the high priest was saying, 'We picked you because we want the loudest rain.' Then I woke up." He turned to me with a quizzical expression. "Wacky, eh?"

My laughter came out in short gasps. It was so unbelievable to me that Mink Lasher should be so close, telling me about his dream, that I scarcely dared to breathe.

After a moment he came over and stood right beside me. "Let me show you something." He led me across the hall to a railing and gestured with his hand. "This is what I like," he said.

Suddenly I noticed that we were on a kind of balcony that

overlooked the club. Below us people danced; next to me was the most amazing man in the world.

It was as if we were standing amidst the stars, gazing out across the universe.

* * *

Ruby looked at the magazine cover and shook her head. "I don't know about that chick," she said, while the band set up behind her in the stage area of Grossman's. "She goes around sleeping with married men, like it's all just a game. And I don't believe in that."

I was surprised to hear Ruby speak that way about Delilah Zed, her longtime friend. Only a few months ago Ruby had told me during one of our chats, "Delilah always puts a smile on my face. She tries to be shocking, but that's really part of her act. She always makes me laugh!"

But now, after seeing "Toronto's Premier Witch," according to the caption, on the cover of the issue of *Dimensions* that I had brought with me that night, Ruby smirked as she flipped through the pages. "Well, let's see what the chick has to say."

I felt chagrined that I had, even inadvertently, brought up a subject distasteful to Ruby. My shame increased when Ruby, after skimming the article for half a minute, shook her head in disgust and set it down. "Some people!" she exclaimed.

I had never before given much thought to the matter of adultery, and had formed no opinion of whether it was right or wrong. But Ruby's clear aversion to it made up my mind, and I was thankful for her sisterly instruction.

Then I remembered something I wanted to ask her. "You said you live in the Beaches?"

"Uh-huh."

"I'm gonna be in that area on Saturday to drop off a paper I need to get typed..."

"Sure! Come on by." She had read my mind. "Just call me that morning, after ten. I should be around."

* * *

The half-hour streetcar ride to Queen Street's east end had taken me into a new realm of the city – past boutiques and cafes, with an occasional glimpse of the frozen beach and, beyond, the chilling austerity of Lake Ontario.

Now, as I mounted the daunting, unshoveled stairs to the one-story house on Neville Park Boulevard, I felt that I was ascending to a higher level of being.

Warmth suffused me as I let myself into the foyer, as Ruby on the phone had directed me to do. A red wooden door beckoned to the right. After a few deep breaths, I knocked.

Something clicked on the other side, and then the door swung open. "Hello!" Ruby, clad in the same sort of lace-and-miniskirt outfit she wore at her gigs, greeted me with a kind smile. "Come awwwn in!" she said, stepping aside.

"Hi!" After taking off my snowy shoes and leaving them on a mat by the door, I made my first entrance into the Lasher-Treece living room.

Although the cream-colored walls, faded carpet, and overstuffed couch looked ordinary enough, the numerous Asian statuettes and colorful silk scarves, together with a pungent incense aroma, gave the place the aura of a temple.

Mink's beige-and-chestnut guitar, worn to the point that its previously sharp edges had become rounded, rested against the side of an easy chair, deceptively tame, like a sleeping dragon.

I presented Ruby with a quart of Haagen-Dazs ice cream I had picked up at a corner store – vanilla, a safe flavor, I thought. Suddenly I was embarrassed to have brought ice cream in the winter.

But Ruby seized it with a childlike glee. "Let's hurry up and eat this before Mink wakes up!" She hurried into the kitchen and returned with a couple of teaspoons and wooden bowls. The ice cream proved too hard to scoop out right away, so we let it sit on the coffee table as we conversed.

"I fasted for five days last week," Ruby told me. "It was just what I needed! I always feel so much more invigorated, so cleansed afterwards."

My experience with anorexia had left me feeling anything but that. "Do you not eat *anything* when you fast?" I asked gravely.

"I don't eat anything solid. But for energy I drink this mixture that a holistic doctor once told me about. It's lemon juice and cayenne pepper and these herbal extracts. It's great!"

It didn't sound like a very good idea to me, but Ruby was beaming with satisfaction. "Mink did even better. He was on it for two weeks! That's longer than I've ever done. He lost a lot of weight, and felt a million times better afterwards."

I felt something nuzzle at my leg. Looking down, I beheld an enormous striped cat. "Nice kittycat!" I exclaimed.

Ruby smiled. "That's Zydeco," she said. "We got him as a stray at the Humane Society down on Queen Street – you probably passed it on your way up here. I didn't even want him at first. We had talked about getting a kitten, and here was this ugly, mangy cat, covered with scars and burns! But Mink latched onto him right away, and wouldn't have any other cat. It was as if they were soulmates! So we had to get him. And almost overnight, he changed into a nice, normal, healthy cat."

As I stroked the animal, who seemed far too large to be described as "normal," I noticed above Ruby's head a sepia-and-white representation of a hooded figure standing amid trees in the gloom of winter. The figure's right arm was outstretched, pointing up towards a glowing white bird. "That's a nice painting," I commented, pointing up myself, like the hooded figure.

"There's an interesting story about that picture," Ruby told me. "I was browsing in an art gallery a few blocks away, and this picture completely captivated me! Then a couple of weeks later, when Mink and I were looking through the gallery together, the picture had the same effect on him, even though I hadn't said anything about it. So we had to buy it! The fact that we were both drawn to this picture – it shows how we're connected on so many levels!" Ruby was glowing, just like the bird.

Once the ice cream had sufficiently melted, we ate, and Ruby continued to tell me the history of various objects in the room. "My mother was visiting us, and she saw that Buddha there, and she said, `Get that devil out of here!' That just indicates how low her consciousness is."

I didn't know exactly what "consciousness" was, but I wanted to know. I wanted to be part of her wondrous, incense-filled realm, and I stayed there, soaking in Ruby's wisdom, until my appointment with the typist loomed dangerously near.

Ruby showed me to the door. "Thanks for coming, Iris." She pecked me softly on the cheek.

"Tell Mink I'm sorry if I made too much noise and woke him up," I said, collecting my scarf and mittens.

Ruby laughed. "No, Mink is dead. Dead to the world!"

* * *

Thursday's issue of *NOW* brought the best possible news. Laird had gotten a kidney transplant.

The Festive Tree exhibit came to Harbourfront again, and elated by the miraculous outcome, I once again paid homage to the Sandalmen tree.

At his next Sunswayers gig, after we had both expressed our joy and relief about Laird, Mink scolded me. "They told us they're gonna give the award to someone else, because it wouldn't be fair otherwise, and that's fine with us." He gave my shoulder a mock punch. "You goof!"

I looked away, devastated.

"So, how was your Christmas?" he asked, raising his voice to be heard above the clamor.

"I...don't know." My thoughts had scattered, but I remembered Ruby saying something about a holiday celebration at their home. "How was your party?"

"Oh, it was great. You should have been there!"

That heartened me a little, and I commented on how crowded the Horseshoe Tavern was that night.

"Crowded?" Mink exclaimed. "It's a *madhouse!*" And it was – people bumped into me as he said it.

"Is Ruby here?" I asked.

He paused to look around. "No," he answered after a moment. "If Ruby were here, I would see her."

He would be able to spot her in a crowd like this? His assertion awed me. I knew that the two of them must share a powerful bond indeed.

But when I was again alone in my room, embarrassment from Mink's reproach haunted me into a nightlong fit of tears. I felt like a kite being blown about in a storm, black clouds all around, with no end in sight.

CHAPTER 6

At the music school, our band conductor singled out a euphonium player for a twenty-minute tirade during one rehearsal. I was shocked and yet at the same time relieved that it wasn't me. Later I heard that the student had consequently dropped out of college and gone back to New Brunswick.

But the nightmares of that world were soon dispelled for me. Ruby had scheduled a video shoot for her song "Lost to the Waves," and had said that I could come. She had even invited me to be in the shoot.

"Joe Bagley and I were talking about you," Ruby had mentioned during the phone call as I tried to absorb all of this incredible information.

Bagley, who had directed two videos for the Sandalmen, was to direct this project as well. I had met him briefly at Grossman's.

"Really?" I felt flattered.

"Yes. He said, `I'm a little afraid of her. She has these great big eyes, and she watches like she doesn't want to miss a thing!'"

It gratified me to know that I had that kind of power over people.

* * *

The Villa stood about forty miles outside the city (I had never learned to think in kilometers). Driving up with Ruby and Mink's friends, albeit in a different car from my two idols, had set my head spinning.

It looked like a Swiss chalet, set on an enormous wooded lot. The outdoor segments were to be filmed later, though. Right now the musicians were downstairs in an airy, cathedral-ceilinged studio so that an actual band session could be captured on film. Ruby, her frizzy-haired friend Tania, and I sat upstairs. The rooms were hooked up with video monitors.

Mink paused in his tuning to glance up at the monitor. "Look, Ruby's smoking a cigarette," he announced with a wicked grin. "Isn't that cute!"

Ruby, who was indeed smoking next to me on the couch, forced a smile. "I only do it about once a month," she told me, apparently feeling a need to explain.

The song "Lost to the Waves," one of her newer ones, told the story of a boy running on the beach, while his footprints got washed away behind him. The message, that one ought to savor every moment before it is gone forever, was presented over a bouncy groove that Mink and the rhythm section were now laying down. Today, vocals would be the last thing done, according to the schedule, so Ruby had time to relax.

"I heard an astrologer on the radio yesterday," she was saying. "He predicted that 1988 would be a good year, since the figure 8, on its side, is the symbol for eternity. So, this year is like 'double eternity'!"

It dizzied me that the numerological forces of the cosmos were on our side, and that I had the privilege of sitting with someone who had such knowledge.

After a while the band took a break, and Mink came upstairs.

"Hey, dear," Ruby said with an exhausted sigh, as if she had been the one playing.

Mink lumbered over to the couch. After kissing each of us on the cheek, he sank to the floor in front of Ruby while she massaged his shoulders.

"When are you gonna do those `ching-a-chang' things?" she asked, mimicking a particular guitar lick he sometimes used.

Mink tensed up visibly. "Aw, Ruby, you should have told me you wanted those. I thought we were done with the guitar tracks already."

"I told you this morning." There was hurt in her voice, but she continued to massage. "It's sounding great, dear. Just throw those down really quickly after lunch, okay? The way we practiced it last week."

Mink grunted in reply.

Eventually, when the two of them were sufficiently rested, we all went down together for a potluck lunch.

The little daughter of the Villa's owner passed us on the stairwell. "You guys both have the same shoes!" she called out, noticing Ruby and Mink's matching cowboy boots.

Ruby laughed. "That's what happens when you get married!" she replied.

Later, when we were seated together at a long table, I asked Ruby, “Are you and Mink really married?” It was news to me if they were.

“No, not officially, but we might as well be. We’ve been together for eight long years.”

“Do you think you ever will `tie the knot’?” Tania asked, her mouth full of banana.

“No, because it wouldn’t change anything.” Ruby stirred her mug of herbal tea. “Of course, if it were up to Mink, we would have been married yesterday. But we can’t even afford to go on a honeymoon, so what’s the point?”

As I pondered this reasoning, Joe Bagley called Ruby over to discuss her plans for the afternoon.

I got up to refill my plate. Paul, the bass player, was helping himself to some tabouli.

“I can’t wait to see this video on MuchMusic!” I piped.

Paul shrugged. “Ruby’s projects have a way of not getting finished.”

Vaguely angry at him for saying that, I took another piece of quiche and suddenly noticed that I had gotten crumbs all over my shirt.

* * *

That afternoon saw us dancing outside in the snow, around a giant tree stump, in what could have been a pagan ritual. What this had to do with waves and sand eluded me, but Joe Bagley deemed it an excellent shoot.

Later we went in, warmed ourselves with coffee and cocoa, and lounged around while Ruby did her vocals. At gigs she usually had a background singer or two, but this time I admired the way she sang all of the harmonies herself, layering the parts so that, to me, it sounded like an angelic choir.

But Ruby wasn’t happy with it. “There’s too much sibilance,” she muttered, looking defeated as her work was played back to her.

They experimented with putting some type of screen in front of the microphone; Ruby liked the effect of that even less. “Why is this happening to me? Why is this happening?" Her bony fingers pressed into her forehead as if to crush it.

Tania tried to comfort her, but got up after several vain attempts and, heading out of the room, announced, "I'll be right back."

After a while she returned, this time with Mink. "Okay, so what the hell is the problem now?" he blasted.

Tania, appearing stunned, whispered something to him, but he brushed past her. "Ya, whatever. She hates it. I know. We have to have a scene every single fucking time." He glared at Ruby. "Oh, great. Cry about it. That's just what we need!"

"You're the one who's making it a scene!" Ruby shouted back. "Besides, no one would have seen that I was crying if you hadn't pointed it out."

Mink froze for a moment and then backed away. "That's true – I'm sorry," he faltered. Looking around at all the people staring at him, he mumbled, "I'm going now." Then he turned to me. "Iris, you wanna come?"

"N-no, I'm going with Ruby and Tania," I answered, since that had been the plan.

"I don't blame you." He grabbed his guitar case and gig bag. "Ciao!"

* * *

The dark, snowy landscape sped past us. "I thought that I was being helpful by going to get Mink," said Tania, at the wheel.

Ruby uttered a mirthless laugh. "He doesn't deal very well with situations like that. He always thinks I'm blaming him. I just didn't like the way my voice sounded. But he always has to take the weight of the world on his shoulders."

"At least he's sorry," Tania offered.

"Oh, I know he feels really bad about what he did. I'll bet he's gonna go out drinking." She snorted. "In fact, that's probably what he's doing right now. Drinking."

It was long after midnight when they dropped me off at the Castle Frank subway station. As I approached, the doors of the station swung open, propelled most likely by the harsh wind but possibly by some other force. It had been quite a day. I sensed that I had entered a different universe, where the ordinary laws of nature no longer applied.

* * *

A harp recital loomed for me in the early spring, and I had to put in longer hours of practice to memorize the difficult pieces that had been thrust upon me. Sharp pains in my shoulders plagued me almost constantly, and I had to take aspirin several times a day.

Similarly, the pointy, high-healed shoes for practice and performance that Peg had selected for me, at my teacher's insistence, tortured me from the moment I put them on. My teacher had persuaded me that I needed to get used to working the harp pedals in these, so I made an effort at first. But soon I found that, like so many of the other directions from her and the rest of my professors, this one was impossible to carry out. One morning, on my way up Davenport to a lesson, my feet cramped so badly that I had to sit down on the frigid sidewalk for a few minutes, even though I had taken off the high heals a full half hour ago and had on comfortable running shoes.

I realized then that this was yet another instance in my college career where it would be necessary for me to disobey, dissemble and lie.

* * *

"Have you ever seen Wally?" Ruby asked me at Grossman's that weekend.

I hadn't.

"I've known him practically forever," she went on, "and he's one of my favorite songwriters."

Wally was a six-foot-plus, hairy-chested bald guy in a tank top, who was at that moment adjusting the microphone to his height. "Thank you," he intoned in a soft, deep growl. "My first song is called 'Ladder to Your Heart.'" A drum machine loop began; he set in with his spasmodic guitar part. *"If I climb a little higher..."* His beat-driven song conjured up primitive images in my mind: we were all in a cave together, staring into flames. Sometimes he would shake his head blurrily from side to side, causing his words to vibrate crazily against the cave walls. We were all there, and hunting had been good.

At the conclusion of his brief set, I was delighted that he planted his massive frame down next to Ruby and across the table from me.

"Wally," Ruby said, "this is Iris, a classical harpist and a very good friend of mine."

He reached over and shook my hand, squeezing it warmly as if he considered me a good friend of his as well.

After the two of them had chatted a bit, complaining about the infamous Grossman's sound system, Ruby excused herself to prepare for her upcoming numbers.

Wally turned to me, nodding quite affably for a barbarian. "Did Ruby say that you were a harpist?"

I muttered something, and then told him how much I had enjoyed his three songs. "The one about the Abominable Snowman was my favorite," I added, half wondering whether he and the mythical beast were related.

Wally beamed, as if my opinion mattered a great deal to him. "Mink's helping me make a demo of those songs right now. Hopefully we'll finish it in the next few months." Then the brightness left his face. "Of course, we're gonna have to put it on hold for a while, since he's going to Mexico."

"Mexico?"

"Yeah, he goes there sometimes..." His fingers began massaging invisible circles into his shiny scalp. "I've tried to talk him out of it...Anyway, Ruby says it'll be good for him to get away, like a vacation. And, God knows, he needs to get healthy again."

I bolted upright. "Is something wrong with him?"

Wally raised an imaginary glass to his lips. "Aah, just too much drinking and partying."

I relaxed again, hugely relieved that it was nothing serious.

Meanwhile, the band had reassembled, and my attention was directed again towards the front of the room.

* * *

With Mink away, there was little for me to do but practice and, periodically, spend late evenings at Peg and Pamela's apartment, munching on pizza or homemade cookies.

My body had begun to take on plump curves, and daily became less recognizable as my own. Already my harp teacher, ever willing to invade my private life, had suggested that I lose weight, but I had my own reason for wanting to do just that. Ruby and Mink, and indeed most in their artistic circle, had such sublimely slender physiques that I felt my new layers of fat weighing me down and barring me from their lighter-than-air bohemian heaven.

Meanwhile, the recital came and went. Then, at last, I could celebrate the return of spring and, with it, the return of Mink.

* * *

The crowd had spilled out onto the stone patio. In front of the Bamboo, a small fountain babbled and splashed, lit with magenta and green lights.

Nearby, Mink was discussing something with Eric, the soundman. After they had clapped each other on the back and Eric had gone into the club, a group of women accosted Mink in boisterous good-humor; apparently familiar with all of them, he chatted for several minutes, roaring in laughter at some comment I had failed to hear.

"Give my best to Ruby," the stout, husky-voiced blonde who had been the loudest, called back as they headed inside. "She's a jewel!"

Once they had gone and I had Mink to myself, I ventured to comment on the breathtaking performance I had just witnessed during the second set.

"That solo in `Sweet Lady of Love' was great!"

Mink held out a joint to me. When, amused, I shook my head, he took a drag. "That was building up inside me the whole time. I kept waiting, thinking, Is it time yet? Is it time yet? And when Jimbo finally signaled to me, I exploded. Ya, I was waiting for that solo all night."

I nodded. "So was I."

Mink shot me a sardonic grin.

"You don't do as many wild solos with the Sunswayers as with your other bands," I commented.

"No, but this is good for me," he said. "Most of the bands that I play in depend on me to do...what I do. Playing with the Sunswayers is good practice for me in just laying back and listening." He took another drag. "Ya, that was hard for me to get used to at first. Because whenever there was a space in the music, I would fill it. And you can't do that in reggae. It just doesn't work."

I would have been quite happy for him to fill in all the spaces, I was going to say, but just then Jimbo motioned to him from the doorway and Mink, patting me on the shoulder, took his leave.

For most of the third set, Mink lingered in the shadows towards the back of the stage, occasionally wandering over to the drummer or the keyboard player in apparent fascination with their playing. My mind went back to his "Sweet Lady of Love" solo, and to the orgasmic zeal of his performance.

At the end of the concert, I sought Mink backstage. "You did a good job of not showing off," I teased him.

Mink twisted his mouth into a grimace. "That's my function in this band, to 'not show off'," he said.

I perceived that he might be growing weary of me, or that he had other things to do. "Just one more thing," I had to add. "The way you play tho guitar, you make it look like it's the most exciting thing in the world."

"Oh, it is!" He almost purred the words.

"I wish I felt that way about the harp, but I just don't."

"Gee..." Mink looked genuinely concerned.

"What's your secret?"

He livened up. This was clearly his favorite subject. "It's because on the guitar, you can play anything you want. It's random notes."

"Yeah, but you know what you're doing."

"No," he said emphatically. "Even if you don't, just play all the strings. DWANG!" He made a sweeping gesture with his hand to illustrate. It made me laugh. "On the harp, or the french horn, or any classical instrument, everything has to be so correct." He gestured again with his hands, holding his arms up stiffly in an uncannily accurate approximation of harp technique. “Right from the beginning, everything has to be exactly a certain way.” He relaxed his arms. “But on the guitar, you just play anything you want. I could come over to your place sometime and we can jam...”

CHAPTER 7

The possibility of Mink coming to my little room at the co-op to "jam," as he had put it, made me nearly feverish. I practiced extra caution in crossing streets and going down stairs, lest my life should be ended before that miraculous event should be allowed to take place.

Mink had another Sunswayers gig at Lee's Palace the next Saturday night, and I thought that might be a good time to pin him down to a specific date and time, to make sure the visit would get beyond the hypothetical stage.

During the first break, I spotted Mink coming out of the club's dining area carrying a plate heaping with meat and vegetables in gravy, wafting a delicious aroma of curry.

I approached him. "So, do you know if you'd have time this week to come by?"

"I can't get anything together here!" he snapped. "Call me at home. I can't get anything together here." His words trailed after me as I turned and retreated. "Call me at home or something."

Numbly I fled, eventually hiding at a table near the wall. I was too stunned to cry and just sat staring at the black tabletop, with its reluctant reflection of light.

I was already well into my pit of misery when someone squeezed my shoulders. I looked up, and Mink was laughing, full of good humor, inviting me to join in his mirth. I couldn't help laughing, too, bewildered as I was.

He gave my shoulder a final squeeze and walked on by.

My tension dispelled, I resettled myself at my former table by the dance floor, as close as I could get to Mink's side of the stage, where his guitars stood ready and eager for their master's return.

* * *

I did as Mink had bidden me and called him at home. I almost couldn't believe it when we settled on the next Wednesday, at two-thirty. He also informed me that Loudest Rain had a gig that very night, filling in for Gwen Swick, a singer who'd had to cancel, at a club in the

Kensington Market area.

So it was that I found myself one storey above Augusta Street, seated at a makeshift desk to collect cover charges for the band. This was my first stint at “doing the door.” Mink had asked me if I would mind doing it since none of his other friends had shown up. Gladly, I had obliged.

“Sorry we didn’t get more people, but it wasn’t my gig,” I heard Mink saying to a hefty man, evidently the club’s owner.

It outraged me that the supreme Mink Lasher had to humble himself this way. I looked down at the cashbox, which was shamefully empty. That was partly my fault; I had turned away a few people who, coming in the middle of the gig, had been unwilling to pay the full three-dollar cover charge. Mink had approached me at some point and told me to let such people in anyway. This policy change was irrelevant, since no one else came.

Both sets had been brilliant. Mink had given his all for the eight people (myself included) in the audience. His solos had soared, and the band had supported him with spirit and savagery. Yet the cashbox declared the gig a failure.

I rummaged through my purse and dug out every bill and coin that I could find. It came to just about fifty-two dollars. Every cent of that I slipped into the cashbox.

Mink came over to count the money. “Iris!” he exclaimed.

I shrunk in my seat.

He sighed. “Let me buy you a grasshopper.”

When I called Mink the next morning to confirm our appointment, his voice was hoarse and crackly. “Sorry, I’m ill. Good thing I could do my gig. I sang my little heart out!” he said, laughing weakly.

We rescheduled for the following Tuesday.

* * *

Tuesday arrived, and Mink was to come at three in the afternoon. At last!

It frustrated me that, in spite of my yearning to make a good impression, I was still unable to get my room into any state resembling order. The mess had never bothered me before, but now, viewing it as Mink might, it seemed intolerable. Yet cleaning was something that I simply couldn't manage. The best I could do was arrange the various papers and newspapers into crude piles on top of and under the two desks, leaving the bed, the chair, and the center of the floor free of clutter. I tried to spread the sheets and blankets as smoothly as I could over the bed, placing my various stuffed animals around the pillow.

Then I noticed the walls. Over my bed was the Sandalmen poster, among the first things one might see upon entering the room. Elsewhere on the walls, scattered about, were articles and photos clipped out of *NOW, Rock Express, The Globe and Mail,* and other publications, mentioning Mink, Ruby, the Sandalmen, or any musicians that I knew had played with them. I even had a picture of Delilah Zed which, even after Ruby's comments, I hadn't been able to bring myself to take down. I panicked. Mink would see all this and become alarmed, think I was a stalker, hate me...

Peg and Pamela had once given me a poster of the two of them, Peg singing and Pamela accompanying her on the piano. I got out my mounting tape and hastily put it up near my bed. What else...maybe some programmes from the concerts I had played in? Notices about disarmament or animal rights events? I dug out items from the piles of paper and mounted my finds on the walls and on the side of my bookcase. Before long it began to look like the room of someone with a wide range of interests – or so I hoped.

Three o'clock came and went. I got up the courage to call, but there was no answer. I sank to the floor in a lump.

At three-thirty the phone rang, and it was Mink's voice on the other end. "Sorry, I'm running a bit late." He chuckled. "I was having a bath. But I'll be there at about four. Is that okay?"

* * *

Almost exactly a half hour later, the buzzer rang. I raced to open the front door.

Mink was on the porch, carrying a large, triangular case. Even standing there he seemed to be part of another realm, a wild bird come to visit this chicken coop.

"C-come in," I said, and stepped aside. After recovering from the shock of seeing him enter, I remembered my role as hostess. "Do you want a beer?" This was not something I normally had on hand, but I had made sure to get some for this occasion.

He elbowed the door shut. "I would love a beer!"

I rushed to the kitchen to grab a cold bottle out of the refrigerator, and then ushered Mink to my room, such as it was.

The humid, summer-like air drifted dustily into the awkward spaces in our conversation.

"Who do you listen to mostly?" I asked.

"Beethoven. Mozart."

I laughed; he was serious.

"Can you read music?"

"Oh ya. I played french horn in high school. But I never got too much into that legit music thing. It was too rigid for me."

By "legit," I realized that he meant "classical." I found it amusing that what I did was "legit," while what he did was...illegitimate? "The music is good, though," I said.

"Oh, the music is unbelievable!" he agreed. "But the training is pretty..." he gestured with his hands to show something square or boxed in. "And that's fine. Some people wouldn't have it any other way," he added, pausing to emphasize the point. "But for me, it's way too rigid."

As unsuited as I was to the classical music scene, I sensed that I had a long way to go to be a part of his world.

"There are a lot of people I meet at the music school who think that anything that isn't classical isn't real music," I commented.

"Ah, the purists." He shook his head. "There are always people like that. In jazz, too. Or even in rock, there are people who don't like anything that isn't Whitesnake." He took a swig of beer.

I tried to think of something else to say. After a moment I asked: "Do your parents approve of what you do?"

"Both my parents are dead," he answered.

I shuddered.

"But they let me do what I wanted," he continued. "They were pretty cool."

There was another pause, during which I reached for one of my long-simmering questions. "Did you always want to be a guitarist?"

"Always," he answered, speaking the word before I had even finished. "Always."

"How did you get started?"

A smile spread over his face as he became enlivened by the memory. "I started when I was thirteen. There was this kid named Kento next door...he was a year older than I was, and he was always in his backyard, blasting his guitar. It was just the greatest sound I had ever heard! So I started playing."

"Cool!"

"Of course," he added with a chuckle, "we also wanted the babes! Ya, Kento and I were really into that whole 'rock thing.' You know, 'sex, drugs, and rock 'n' roll'!"

It amused me to imagine Mink as a young boy, full of wild and crazy dreams. His last remark, though, reminded me of something. I hesitated, biting my chapped lip, and then asked: "When you go on your trips to Mexico, is it...is it about drugs?"

To my surprise, he threw his head back in laughter. "I wish it were!" Then he became more serious. "It's about feeding the hungry."

I would have expressed my admiration, but a pall seemed to have fallen over the room.

Finally breaking the spell of silence, Mink said, "Play another tune."

"Okay..." I moved the music stand closer, embarrassed that I needed one, that I was so dependent on the printed page. I had already played one piece for him, and had avoided botching it too badly. Now, as I embarked upon the slow movement of a sonata, I hoped that my luck would hold up again.

Out of the corner of my eye I could see that Mink had his eyes closed and was swaying in rhythm to my playing. I breathed deeply to keep from shaking.

After I had concluded my little performance, Mink clapped energetically. “Bravo!” he exclaimed, utterly flattering me.

It felt for a minute as if we were truly colleagues. “So,” I asked, “how do you improvise, to come up with your unbelievable solos?” I realized immediately that it was a stupid question, but I wanted an answer.

Mink sighed. “My playing is the result of years of experience,” he said.

Obviously that was true, but it left me dejected. I had hoped that he could give some pointers to steer me in the right direction.

Perhaps he sensed this. “It’s all really based on the blues scale,” he told me, his voice taking on a sudden gravity to highlight this principle. “All of rock is based on the blues.”

I sat rapt in attention as he began to explain rudimentary blues theory to me. Music theory had long been the bane of my existence, but here under his guidance I relished it, especially when he brought out his guitar to demonstrate. “So you have scale degrees one, three, four, five, flat-seven, and then one again, on top...” He suffered my first awkward attempts to imitate this on the harp, encouraging me with an occasional “Ya...yup.”

When he seemed satisfied that I was at last getting the hang of it, he began to strum a basic blues accompaniment, sending ecstatic shivers down my spine.

After a few minutes of this he put down his guitar, stood up, and came towards the harp. “Here, mind if I try?” He set his beer down on my table and, as I eagerly made way for him, sat down on the harp stool. “What are the notes on this thing?”

I had barely finished two sentences of reply about the layout of the strings when he started doing his own blues improvisation on it, singing along with each note as he played it. When he concluded with a flashy trill, we both burst out laughing, myself mainly out of an eerie sense of wonder that already he could play my instrument more freely than I could.

“So,” he said, setting the harp upright again and standing up, "get yourself a blues record and put it on. That's the best way to start with the whole improvising thing."

His attention turned to the posters on my walls. Far from being alarmed, he positively lit up as he noticed a photo of Delilah Zed with tiara and wand. "Isn't she wacky?" he exclaimed, scrunching up his face into a comical grimace. He skimmed over a printed music review or two, and then turned, flashing me an indulgent grin. "Do you spend most of your time in your room?" he asked.

I nodded and looked down, terribly embarrassed that he had perceived the truth.

"Oh, I should probably call Ruby," he said. "Do you have a phone?"

I pointed to the little white one on the dresser.

"Thanks." Those magical, slightly stubby fingers that so often had me mesmerized with their guitar mastery now pressed the buttons of my telephone. As he listened, waiting for Ruby to answer, I realized that I was standing very close to him. It scared me, and I took a few steps back while he made his call.

After he hung up, he glanced at his watch. "I oughtta get going soon – I don't want to get caught in the middle of rush hour." Maybe he saw my face sink. "Play one more tune," he requested.

When, inevitably, the time did come for him to leave, I thanked him and showed him to the door. Then, returning to my room, I tried as best I could to absorb what had just happened.

To my amazement, the space where Mink had sat felt much hotter than the surrounding area.

The beer bottle from which he had drunk still stood on my table. It remained there for over a month, until patches of mold grew on the bottom.

CHAPTER 8

I was disappointed about having to depart for summer vacation just as the city was at its most vibrant, but not as disappointed as I might have been. Ruby's video project had met with unforeseen complications, and at present, things had been put on hold.

As Ruby explained to me when I phoned one evening, it would be necessary for her to track down the artists who had done some paintings that appeared in her video, to get permission to show their work. As if that were not hassle enough, Joe Bagley had been called away on business and would be unavailable for the next two months at least.

So, as I languished in Ann Arbor, I had the consolation of imagining that I wasn't missing too much in Toronto, that my group was frozen in place, waiting for me.

* * *

The deliciously smoke-filled Grossman's air greeted me one blessed Saturday night in September.

"Do you ever watch those assholes in Parliament?" Standing amidst a small group of regulars, Mink grunted and grumbled, mimicking the Parliamentarians. "What a joke! What are they even doing there?"

"It's because they all represent the rich special interests..."

"They represent no one!" Mink interrupted, waving his hand disdainfully at the young man who had spoken. "That's the problem. They're an absurd entity unto themselves. Parliament right now is just a remnant of British sovereignty. It has nothing to do with Canada."

I sneaked past, making my way to the women's room at the back. Elated as I felt to be here again, my nervousness had me almost nauseated, and I would need a few minutes alone to summon up my courage.

I stood at the sink, fiddling with the contents of my purse, pretending to look for something...

"Iris! I thought that was you I saw ducking in here!" Ruby's warm smile beamed at me in the mirror, and I spun around to face her.

It was the first time I had seen her since I had come back, and my joy and shyness tripped me up so that I was at a loss for words.

Ruby squeezed my shoulder. "So, how was your summer?"

"Oh, good...how was yours?"

"Hot!" she exclaimed with a laugh. "Way too hot! It just made me realize that we really need a new place. Where we live, it's so small – oh, you've been there. Especially in the heat, I feel so crammed in there, with Mink. I just need more room to air out!"

"You look gorgeous, as always!" I said. And she did. Her eyes startled me with their blue-gray wisdom, sparkling in the dim bathroom light. Her hair, somewhat shorter than usual, brushed against the leopard-spotted scarf she had knotted around her graceful neck.

"Oh..." She squeezed my shoulder. "Well, we'll talk later. I have to go get ready. We're doing a couple of songs that I just wrote, and I want to go over the lyrics again."

"Can't wait to hear 'em!"

She left and I followed soon after, reclaiming my seat near the front. As I opened up the copy of *NOW* that I had grabbed on the way in, the waiter set down a grasshopper in front of me, and I thanked him with a grateful laugh. Out of the corner of my eye I noticed Levi, the drummer, sitting further down the long table. Curious about everyone connected with my group, I focused my attention on him to eavesdrop, while pretending to read the magazine.

"Yeah, well...That's pretty typical," I heard him say to the fellow next to him, who muttered an unintelligible response. Levi snickered and went on: "Actually, I don't know what I'm doing, wasting my time in this band. What I'm really into now is Madonna. I think she's great! I could listen to her all day. I'm sick of this indie shit."

Hunched over my magazine, I sat there, dumbfounded by his treachery. When the band went onstage, I avoided looking at him, since he had clearly forfeited his right to be there.

The new songs went well enough. One of them, as Ruby explained from the microphone, was a sharp denunciation of diplomatic immunity for a killer; the other, a humorous portrayal of a neighbor who talked too much. But the highlight of the evening, for me, came in the last set during one of the band's older songs, "Light Me, Love Me," when Mink suddenly appeared charged with some mysterious current, playing with such a powerful surge of energy that the other musicians cleared the area as if to avoid getting a lethal shock.

Even after the band had finished and I had gotten up, used the bathroom, and taken my leave of Ruby, my body felt numb and spent just from witnessing such a performance.

Suddenly Mink's arms were around me in a bear hug. It was the warmest place in the world. "Thanks for coming, Iris," he said, kissing me on top of the head and releasing me.

"You know, it's really scary how great you are!" I managed to get out.

He smiled, possibly embarrassed, but willing to accept the tribute. "That last set was pretty good," he acknowledged. "The first two were horrible, though."

"I liked them!"

"No," he explained, "I mean, they were horrible for me." He elaborated a bit: the audience hadn't been with it, the band hadn't been together, the beer hadn't kicked in yet...whatever the reason, we both knew that it was something besides his playing which had fallen short. I didn't see this as arrogance; he was merely recognizing the obvious: that he was a phenomenal musician. It was simply a fact.

I walked home from Grossman's, communing with the stars, past decaying brick buildings that dissolved into the night.

* * *

Always it weighed upon me that this would be my final year in Toronto. Despite my negligence as a student, I was scheduled to graduate in the spring, and my student visa would expire shortly thereafter.

I had inquired about the possibility of getting landed immigrant status. This could be accomplished, I had learned, if one possessed skills that were in great demand, or if one had a definite job offer – or, perhaps, if one married a Canadian. None of these conditions had much likelihood of applying to me. I could not even remain here for graduate school, since my mediocre grades disqualified me from that. As fervently as I wished it were otherwise, my days in this paradise appeared numbered.

Meanwhile, I mechanically went through the process of applying to other graduate schools. My first choice was the University of Michigan, in my hometown of Ann Arbor. There I would at least have familiar surroundings to help ease the pain I knew I would experience after leaving Toronto. I also had been told that I had a good chance of being accepted there. That being the case, I didn't put much effort into applying elsewhere, although I did fill out the forms for two or three other institutions.

On a particularly windy day, when I was trying to stuff an application to one of these less-preferred schools into a mailbox along Bloor Street, a strong gust snatched it away. A nearby pedestrian chased after it, and when his attempts to catch it for me failed, seemed to feel much sorrier than I did.

* * *

Wally, whom I had often seen perform during intermissions at Grossman's, had landed a gig of his own at the Cameron on Queen Street, a few blocks west of Spadina. "I don't have anything with the band coming up," Ruby told me on the phone, "but I'll be going to see him. Mink's gonna be playing guitar, and I'll be doing background vocals on a couple of the songs."

I didn't keep her for long, regretting that I had obviously woken her up. But it gratified me to have this information.

The following Wednesday night I entered the club, where a few young patrons lounged at the bar. Their leisurely mood sharply contrasted with my own almost unbearable excitement. My heart raced in my chest when I heard the music blasting from a back room. I hurried toward the doorway, paid a five-dollar cover charge, inserted my ear plugs, and entered the shadowy, smoke-filled den.

The stage was right by the entrance. There was Mink, his hand a frenzied blur of funk grooves as Wally, in a tank top, leaped about on the small stage as an ape might have done had it tried to dance.

I lingered near the door until my eyes grew accustomed enough to the dark for me to locate an empty seat. I found one close to the front and sank into it, my heart still pounding.

Following a brief applause, the band began another song, Mink's hand again nearly invisible with motion. He stood rapt with concentration near the wall, hardly centerstage but the center of my vision nonetheless. As I sat there, I distinctly perceived a golden aura about him, as if he had been specially highlighted for me.

During break, I congratulated Wally and then situated myself beside Ruby. "I didn't see you!" I exclaimed, setting my cumbersome purse at my feet.

"That's because I just got here. I'm not on until the second set."

I had to keep scooting in closer to the table to allow people in the aisle past. Ruby's gaze had drifted off, and I wanted to keep her attention. "Next Friday is Laird's birthday," I told her, remembering the date from an article on the Sandalmen that I had once read.

She perked up. "Oh, thanks for reminding me. We try to call him or send a card. Last year we forgot, and felt terrible about it afterwards."

The second set didn't last long, since Wally was sharing the gig with another band. However, I was pleased to hear the song about the Abominable Snowman in a more complex arrangement, with Ruby supplying some dissonant vocal harmonies and Mink hamming it up on guitar.

After the set, Ruby sat by me again while I raved about her singing, only to be drowned out by all the noise.

Mink, surrounded by a small cluster of men, moved slowly towards us, occasionally bursting into a roar of laughter. Upon reaching Ruby, he swooped down and kissed her cheek. Then, standing up again, he boasted to the guys, "Didn't I tell you she was the prettiest woman here?"

I moved aside as Mink pulled up a chair. "Thanks, man," he said, shaking hands with each of his buddies, who then disappeared into the murky depths of the club. Mink sat down next to Ruby and, kissing her again, pressed her to his side.

"Your hand must feel like rubber!" I shouted at him over the din.

"Like what?" he shouted back.

"Rubber!"

He smiled vaguely and turned back to Ruby. Sensing that they needed some privacy, I pulled out my book. But it was too dark to read, so after a few moments I got up to use the washroom.

When I returned, my seat had been taken, and Mink had once again amassed a small group of people around him. "You don't want to know what's going on in my head," he was saying. "Guitar thoughts – bee-oo-wee-ngayouonggg!" He laughed.

I moved in closer, picking up what I could of the animated conversation, but mostly content just to watch. When a couple of the people had dispersed, Mink scooped Ruby up onto his lap as I had seen him do before. As she looked up, her eyes caught mine. "Oh, hi, Iris," she said, her manner uninhibited, as if sitting on someone's lap in public were the most natural thing in the world for a grown woman to do.

"So, should I call to remind you about Laird's birthday?" I asked, preparing once more to leave.

She snuggled closer to Mink. "Yes, call to remind."

"Call to remind," he echoed, his eyes squinting at me through the smoke. The two of them had the same dreamy grin, as if they were both posing for me to remember them that way, in that drunken state of bliss.

* * *

When I did call the following week, Ruby let me know of a newly-scheduled gig she had coming up at Grossman's. She seemed particularly excited about it, telling me that she hoped to try out some unusual styles of vocal harmony, partly influenced by her exposure to the music of the Bulgarian Women's Chorus. The evening, she predicted, would take her in a totally new direction.

I noticed that *NOW* had a band called Flying Debris listed for Grossman's on the night in question, and I even called the tavern to ask about that. After the woman who answered verified the information in

NOW, I phoned Ruby back to make sure I had the correct date.

"The sixteenth...yes, that's right." Her lyrical voice put me at ease, and I assumed that the other woman must have been mistaken. Loath to take up any more of Ruby's time than necessary, I said goodbye without mentioning the fact that there was a discrepancy between her information and that of the other two sources.

I had forgotten about the incident until we all showed up at Grossman's, only to find another band indeed scheduled for that night. How the mix-up occurred I never understood; however, my own failure to prevent the disastrous outcome stands out vividly in my mind.

It ended up with Ruby, Tania and me huddled around a table in a Vietnamese restaurant across the street, while Mink and the rest of the band stayed at Grossman's to have drinks with the members of Flying Debris.

Ruby rocked back and forth in her chair, eyes closed, muttering, "Why is this happening to me? Does it mean that I'm not supposed to perform anymore? Is that what I'm supposed to learn from this?"

Ever the Pollyanna, I suggested, "No! It means you're supposed to get *more* gigs, so that if this happens once in a while, it won't matter so much."

But she seemed not to hear me. Even with Tania at her side, offering words of encouragement, Ruby kept up her compulsive rocking, now repeating in a whisper, "It's a sign, I know it is. It's a sign. It's a sign."

CHAPTER 9

Eagerly I awaited the completion of the video. I envisioned it being played on the MuchMusic channel, and had come up with several imaginary introductions with which the video jockeys might precede it.

However, when there was no word of it, and after Ruby had dodged the subject on a couple of occasions when I had tried to bring it up, I gathered that the endeavor had been tabled for the time being.

I believe it was around that time that my parents divorced. Although I had feared all my life that this would happen, somehow the news brought me a deep sense of relief. It meant a long-overdue end to the fighting, the insults, and the humiliation.

* * *

The Sunswayers were booked for two nights at a downtown club I had never heard of, called the Tangerine. Since I had to play an orchestra concert in another city, I couldn't make the first night, but made sure to get there early for the second one.

The pleasantly bright, modern interior of the basement-level club struck me as a refreshing change from the dinginess of Grossman's. I ordered at the bar, settling for a fuzzy navel instead of the unavailable grasshopper, and after meandering around for a few minutes, leaned back against a partition and sipped my drink.

Mink appeared beside me. "Weird place, isn't it?"

I hadn't found it particularly weird. "I like the fish!" I chimed in.

Mink looked over at a large, fluorescent-lit tank where enormous goldfish swam about. "They're probably the happiest things in this place," he remarked.

A billiard game was going on to our right. Inane banter from the players, all dressed in sport jackets or suits, drifted towards us.

I felt Mink's hand on my shoulder. "Let's go over there. Too many yuppy businessmen here for me," he said, steering me to a small table on the other side of the room.

I noticed that he had an intriguing haircut. Dark and straight, his hair hung almost at shoulder length, with a single thin lock allowed to grow a few inches longer, down the center of his back. I had never seen this style before; perhaps he or Ruby had invented it.

"Did you have to pay?" he asked apologetically once we were seated. "I have your name on the guest list – you can get your money back."

"No, it's Ladies' Night, so I got in free."

He smiled.

"So, is Ruby coming here tonight?" I inquired.

"No, she won't be down here. Actually, maybe I shouldn't be telling you this, but she has really bad menstrual pains."

"I know. She told me."

Mink's expression became tortured, as if he were the one experiencing the pain. "She often gets those. The way she described it to me, it's as if someone were to put my nuts in a vice and then squeeze them...how awful!"

As crude as the analogy was, his sensitivity impressed me. "A lot of men don't believe it when women talk about that," I commented.

"You've got to believe it," Mink insisted. Then he looked at me gravely. "If you're going out with a guy and he doesn't believe you, don't go out with him anymore. Don't even talk to him."

I could hardly stand to think of being with any other guy, even a hypothetical one. Still, his concern for my welfare touched me, almost to the point of tears. He was so unusual, so unbelievably sympathetic for a man.

A moment passed, filled with the sounds of sporadic billiard shots and an occasional cheer. I took a few sips and then set my glass down to ask: "How was last night's gig?"

"Good. We had a pretty big audience – unlike tonight," he said, casting a sneering glance at the room. "Fridays are always better than Saturdays."

"Why is that?"

"It's because Friday night everyone gets off from work and wants to go out and party. Saturday, people spend the whole day lying around drinking beer," he said, his hand lifting an imaginary bottle to his lips, "and if they go out to a club that night, they have no energy."

I found it amusing that such a generalization could be found to be true.

"Do you have any Loudest Rain gigs coming up?" I asked.

"Naw. I do a lot better in other people's bands – I'm too lazy to go around calling clubs to get gigs..." Abruptly he stopped. "You shouldn't touch your face so much," he said.

I suddenly became aware that my chin was resting in my hand. Blood rushed hotly to my face, and I quickly dropped the offending hand.

"I notice that when I touch my face a lot," he explained, "I get blemishes."

Conscious at once of the blackheads and puss pimples sprinkled across my face, I couldn't concentrate on whatever conversation we had after that.

It came time for the set to begin. Mink grabbed his beer and went onstage, while I miserably nursed what was left of my fuzzy navel.

* * *

Ruby's band had an upcoming gig at a prominent Queen Street club called the Rivoli.

I made posters for the event – five hundred copies, as opposed to my ucual two hundred – xeroxed on neon yellow paper from the original, a crude sketch I had drawn of a band on a stage, with a background of twinkly stars. In the course of a couple of days I managed to put up nearly all of them, pounding the pavement to tape them up until sharp pains plagued my knees and shoulders, and I felt myself on the point of fainting. It gave me great pride to be able to suffer in this way for my cause.

I succeeded in getting a fellow harp student named Cleo to go to the club with me, and we grabbed a table near the front. Unlike Peg or Pamela, Cleo swayed to the beat and even applauded Mink's spastic solos, during one of which he came so close to the edge of the stage that I was afraid he might fall off.

At the end of the concert, though, I left Cleo by herself at the table while I headed backstage to say goodbye to everyone.

I had never seen Ruby so upset. This time, despite my presence and that of Marilyn, her keyboardist, she was actually weeping. From her broken speech between sobs I gathered that the cause of her dismay had to do with that night's performance: the band had been much too loud, despite the fact that during soundcheck she had gone around telling everyone to turn down the volume. She was especially displeased with Mink – as always, the loudest in the band. "He never listens to me. *He never listens to me!*" she wailed, as Marilyn and I stood about helplessly.

It seemed to me that her distress was all out of proportion to the problem, if there even was a problem. As far as I was concerned, the evening's show had been a transcendent experience. Mink's playing, which had so offended her, had excited me, had torn me open in a wonderful way.

But I commiserated with Ruby: "Maybe your next gig will go better."

"I'm not even sure if I want to do another gig," she moaned.

Cleo had already left by the time I got back to our table, so I took the bus home alone.

* * *

Over winter vacation I became acquainted with my father's new apartment, a mile or so away from the family home where I stayed with my mother.

When I got back, January and February went by in a muddle of practicing for my final recital in the spring. Mink had gone to Mexico again, so the gig scene lay stagnant. The weather, although far milder than that of previous Toronto winters I had experienced, felt bitterly cold to me. So I stayed in my room, plucking away, with MuchMusic or CFNY on in the background for company.

When Mink came back in the spring, I rejoiced as if my soul were thawing out. But my celebration was always tempered with a heavy sadness at seeing my last spring in Toronto.

* * *

Frank Prather, a local songwriter whose name I had seen on

posters from time to time, had a gig at the Horseshoe Tavern, and had asked Mink to play in his band for the night.

When I got to the club, I noticed Mink sitting on a stool with his back to the bar, looking forlorn. When he saw me, his face brightened and he kissed my cheek. "How're you doin'?" he asked, putting his arm around my waist.

"I got accepted to the University of Michigan," I told him.

"That's fabulous!" Suddenly he looked very somber. "Then you'll be leaving Toronto?"

"Yeah, I guess so." I hated to think of that. "If I can, though, I'm gonna get an extension on my student visa. They said maybe I could stay through the summer."

His brow was furrowed in thought. "It would be good if you could stay," he said.

* * *

I did get to stay. It took a trip to the Immigration office, with the attendant bureaucracy, but once I got to the window the man seemed eager to accommodate me. My previous experiences with Immigration had hardly been pleasant, and it was such a relief that this procedure had gone smoothly that I actually found myself singing on my way back to the subway.

After graduation freed me from the University of Toronto for good, the city burst into summer and I was there.

* * *

Ruby pored through the magazine, as if hoping to transport herself into one of the dream houses pictured within. "I have such a craving for beautiful surroundings," she said. Her fingers stroked a photo of an amber-cushioned sunroom, which looked rather gaudy to me. Then she flipped to another page, where there was pictured an aquamarine bathroom overlooking an unnamed bay. "These homes are so lovely," she murmured wistfully.

I failed to see the appeal of any of the ritzy mansions in the photographs, when compared to the funky and exotic paradise that was Ruby's own home.

Tania hadn't arrived yet. It was her birthday, and we had arranged to meet for lunch at a cafe in the Eaton Center since Ruby had a voice-over session in the area. ("Not for a movie or anything, just narration for some industrial video," she had explained to me, but it still sounded glamorous.) Meanwhile, we were lingering at a newsstand, killing time.

After a few minutes she replaced the magazine, looking genuinely disappointed to be here instead of in one of the luxury houses. She frowned at her watch. "Tania is always late. It bugs me," she grumbled. "It really bugs me."

Tania finally did arrive, and we had a nice enough lunch of deli sandwiches in the food court. But even though Ruby livened up considerably to gossip with her pal, including me in the conversation from time to time, I couldn't shake the suspicion that she viewed me as part of the drab surroundings from which she would have given anything to escape.

* * *

One Friday night in June I hopped on a subway train after an orchestra concert to catch Mink playing at the Bamboo in a funk outfit called Chazzarre.

"Wishin' fo' yo' love," belted the lean black singer, gripping the microphone with both his hands as the band jammed into a frenzy behind him.

I pushed forward, getting as close to the front as I could. I was still worming my way through the mass of people at the song's abrupt conclusion and during the subsequent cheers and applause. When I saw Mink step forward to start the next song, I stopped.

Pulsating with every muscle in his sweat-drenched body, he laid down a groove that was so rock-solid that I got the sense he was merely responding to a beat that had always been there, of which the rest of us had previously been unaware. Once the band joined in he stepped aside, still locked into the relentless groove.

Later in the set, he actually jumped off the stage and played a solo right in the middle of the dance floor, making me ache with envy of those fortunate enough to watch from up close.

When the band took a break, I stood more or less in place, waiting for the crowd to thin out a little. As I debated with myself whether to order a drink yet or go over to the stage, I saw Mink weaving his way through the crowd only a few feet away from me. When he was within reach, I squeezed his shoulders from behind as he had so often familiarly done to me.

Mink turned around, a startled and aggressive look on his face. When he saw it was me, he forced a smile and continued on his way.

Surrounded on all sides as I was, I had an excuse for the paralyzing inertia that overtook me.

When I was at last able, I wandered over to the bar and ordered a fuzzy navel. Glass in hand, I drifted with the general flow out onto the patio. The wet smacking of the fountain blended with street noises and the hum of conversations all around me.

Mink tapped my arm. "Go call Ruby," he said, handing me a quarter.

Jolted back to life, I obeyed. Entering the Bamboo snack shop which housed the club's pay phone, I waited a few minutes for a tall, sinewy man in dreadlocks to finish his call. Then I dialed the familiar number.

"Hello?"

"Hi, this is Iris."

"Hi there."

"Mink just wanted me to call to see if you were gonna make it here tonight."

"Ah...no, I'm settled in for the night. My energy level isn't up right now. I think I'll just read for a while and go to bed."

"That's too bad. I was hoping I'd see you."

"Well, I'm just not up to it tonight. Thanks for calling, though."

Ruby's "energy level" was apparently a finite, tangible thing, like mercury in a thermometer. I never thought about my energy level. Maybe I didn't have one.

I went back out to the patio to tell Mink the bad news. "She doesn't think she'll be able to make it. She's feeling tired."

He nodded and held out a joint for me, which I declined.

"Are you gonna be at Ruby's gig on Thursday?" I asked him.

"Oh ya, I'll be there." He took a drag and looked away. "I just missed the gig last week because I was on tour with the Sunswayers. That's all it was."

He had indeed missed her gig at Grossman's, which had hence seemed lackluster to me. But I had known about the tour, and that wasn't what I meant. Ruby had recently let me in on one of her ideas that I found quite disturbing. I pried a bit more: "Ruby said she was thinking of having a smaller band."

It was as if I had hit him; Mink winced and recoiled. "I need to give her more space," he muttered. I wasn't certain whether he was talking to me or to himself. Then he looked directly at me. "Yes, I will be playing in the band."

"That's good." We were allies, he and I.

"Let's go inside," he said. We left behind the clear night sky as I followed him into the shadowy mass of writhing figures inside the club.

* * *

When Mink did indeed show up with Ruby at Grossman's that Thursday night, all my apprehensions faded away like bad dreams.

Over the random, eerie howls of his guitar warm-up, I could hear the voices of men down the table from me discussing the Sunswayers.

"You've got Burton, the band's rhythm guitarist, and he's strictly reggae. Then Mink comes into the band, playing like some kind of alien from Mars!"

Soon their conversation was drowned out by soundcheck noises, and shortly after, the show began.

Although this was officially Ruby's gig, she left the stage during the third set, leaving Mink to finish up with a couple of numbers he usually did with Loudest Rain, which this band appeared not to know. While the players faked their way through, joking among themselves about their obvious confusion, Mink peered out into the audience, his eyes baggy and drooping as if weighted down by some extreme form of gravity.

"There's Ruby Treece," he called from the microphone, "the wondrous one. Come up here, Ruby, and sing with us!"

Ruby turned away, her face contorted as I had never seen it before. I pondered this for a moment, but then Mink launched into a guitar solo, and my attention was again riveted to the front.

* * *

Delilah Zed, a fortune-teller as well as a Wiccan priestess, read tarot cards for a small fee in her apartment on Queen Street West. Having seen her ad in *NOW* several times and been curious, I finally called and set up an appointment.

On the designated day I arrived, all ready to have the secrets of the future revealed to me.

"Come in, come in!" Donned in full witch regalia, she beckoned to me as she swung open the door.

Cryptic symbols on posters and cloth hangings covered the walls. Thick black curtains remained drawn over the windows. We sat down together at a low wooden table in the middle of the dimly-lit room. After what I assumed was a brief prayer in some other language, she picked up the tarot deck and said, baring her teeth in a broad smile, "Let's see what the cards have to say."

Cups, pentacles, the hanged man...the room seemed to grow darker, not lighter, though my eyes should have already had time to adjust. "The Sun card," she commented, licking her lips. "That's good – I think."

There would be death. A rebirth. I needed to spend more time around water.

"And you must allow your feminine self to shine through. Those clothes you're wearing now – " She proceeded to ridicule each item of clothing I had on, which hurt me, since I had tried to dress nicely for her, picking out a lavender tank top and velour pants with a floral print.

"Wear only natural fabrics," she instructed me. "Let the Earth herself cover you."

At the end of our session, she told me to visit any of Toronto's numerous New Age bookshops. "Find a book there. You'll know which one. It'll help you on your path."

I did as she suggested, stopping on my way home at a store on Harbord Street that I had passed many times before. After browsing for quite a while, I settled upon a manual for channeling one's spirit guide.

Later, in my room at the co-op, I tried the mental exercises described in the book. I wasn't sure if I was doing them right, though – my spirit guide always looked like Mink, whether we were in a boat, a forest, or an open field. He was always there in front of me, leading the way.

CHAPTER 10

I clung to Toronto with my whole being. Daily I would take long walks, hoping in this way to imprint myself indelibly on the streets and sidewalks of the city. Life couldn't be so cruel as to rip me away from my paradise. Something or someone would surely intervene, like the *deus ex machina* phenomenon we had studied in opera class.

During one of my walks, I discovered a new copying place on Bloor Street that had a much wider selection of colors than most stores. Bright yellow or lime green were my colors of choice for making band posters, because I believed that the black ink stood out most clearly on these. Still, the many fluorescent shades of paper tempted my eye. As a lover of purple, I could hardly resist "molten magenta," "fiery fuchsia," and "vibrant violet." I would definitely keep these in mind for the next Ruby or Loudest Rain gig.

Meanwhile, the Sunswayers were scheduled to play at Harbourfront that Friday night. I never put up posters for them, because they, being a more established band, always had plenty of professionally-done posters already made up and plastered all over Queen Street.

It had been months since I had been to Harbourfront, and that last time had been for a poetry reading by Eddie Noel. Sadly, it hadn't included any performance by the Lipkids, that entity having apparently disintegrated. Still, I always enjoyed being in the company of anyone associated with my group, and the poetry had been quite memorable and witty.

I always had trouble finding my way around Harbourfront, so when Friday came around, I made sure to get there extra-early. This meant waiting around for what seemed like forever in the airy, echo-filled hallways once I had found the correct room, which was locked as yet.

At long last I could hear sounds of the band inside; they had apparently gone in through another entrance. I asked the woman who had stationed herself in front of the door if she could let me in, but she turned me away. Dejected, I continued to roam the halls like a ghost.

Then, suddenly, there was Mink. "Hey, whatcha doin'?" he asked, clapping me on the back.

I laughed, and then told him about my being thwarted by the woman at the door.

"Come on. I'll tell her you're with me," he said.

Heartened, I followed him, no longer feeling like a spirit adrift but rather like one bound for heaven.

"Hey, Bev," he said, embracing the doorkeeper, who now seemed congenial. The two of them exchanged a few pleasantries, and then, under Mink's protection, I was permitted to enter the auditorium.

Mink walked ahead of me towards the stage, where his red guitar was already set up.

"Is Ruby coming?" I called from behind.

"No!" he snapped, and I was taken aback by his tone. Then, in a milder voice, he added: "You know, she doesn't come to very many of these things."

I whimpered in response.

We approached the stage but, once it became clear that there was to be no band action for the time being, we drifted over to a table instead and sat down. Mink already had a big plastic cup of beer, and he offered me a sip. I accepted.

After a few moments had passed in silence, I summoned enough nerve to bring up a subject to him. "Well, anyway, this is a tape of some of my harp tunes that I made up," I said, handing him the crude demo I had cobbled together in my room.

"Thanks!" He picked it up and fingered it, as if that could tell him something about its contents.

"So," I continued, "I was wondering if you could sometime get me a tape of some of your music. I mean, I have the Sandalmen album and the Sunswayers album, but none of your own songs."

He knotted his brow as if deep in thought. "Sure. Sure, I can get you a tape. In fact, maybe you could come down to my studio sometime. I just got a new computer – a new Mac – and I've been having a lot of fun writing stuff on it."

This information surprised me, since I had considered him solely a guitarist. "That would be great! Especially since I'll be going back to Michigan before long, and I want to remember what you guys sound like." It gave me a lump in my throat just to mention that.

But Mink appeared to be contemplating something. "When will you be leaving?" he asked.

"In six weeks," was my gloomy reply.

"Six weeks..." He pondered this for a minute. "Good. That'll give me an excuse to finish a couple of the tunes before then."

It hadn't been the reaction I was hoping for. I struggled not to be crushed.

* * *

It was with unusual ferocity the following Tuesday that I put up posters for Loudest Rain's upcoming performance at the Silver Dollar, and I ventured along King Street as well as the usual Queen, Bloor, and Spadina. By the end of my mission, my knees throbbed with agony, and I treated myself to the services of the Toronto Transportation System on the way home.

As the streetcar jostled along King Street towards the subway station, I had an intense image that became a physical sensation in the pit of my belly, of a cozy, fire-lit room where Ruby and Mink lived, as if they actually dwelled inside of me. I savored the feeling for the duration of the ride.

* * *

"What are you reading?"

Mink had materialized across the table from me.

I handed him my book. "Are you reading anything?" I asked, as if perfectly at ease.

"Actually, I'm reading a science fiction book right now. What's it called...?" Turning slightly to one side, he tipped his head back and closed his eyes, trying to recollect. The position struck me as regal. "Well," he said at length, "it's by a woman."

"Then it must be good!" I asserted.

"Then it must be good!" he said, mimicking me, and laughed.

It was such an uncanny experience watching Mink play that night. How could he possibly have known that each note, each subtle inflection of his expansive solos would so dazzle me with its perfection, as if on some unconscious level I had been craving for him to play it just that way?

"So, which set did you like better: the first or the second?" he asked me jovially after the show. There had been no third set that evening.

While I struggled to decide, he leaned over and kissed my cheek.

I noticed a pendant around his neck, bearing what appeared to be the image of a snake or a bird, like some kind of magical amulet. The thought of something resting against his skin sent such a jolt of excitement through me that I almost jumped.

"You were great!" I gushed with a nervous laugh. As I started to walk away, I felt Mink's hand on my shoulder.

"Oh, by the way," he said, "your tape is fabulous!"

I could feel myself blushing. "You still have to give me a tape of your computer stuff," I reminded him.

"Yes, I do." He sat down on the edge of the stage. "We'll do a trade," he said, his tone disproportionately serious as he considered this.

"Well, see you next time," I said, walking backwards but unable to take my eyes off him, transfixed by the power of his gaze.

* * *

Ruby and Mink seemed genuinely sad that I was leaving, and treated me with greater solicitation than usual. This encouraged me, as I had often been tormented by the notion that I might be deluded, mistaking these inscrutable beings for true friends. Apparently it was no mistake.

I was especially moved when they invited me, over the phone, to see Mink's studio one afternoon, and then to go to their house later and spend the night.

Mink gave me directions to the studio: "You take the Queen streetcar to – what is it? – the Coxwell exit. Then you walk east along the street – you'll pass a couple of little streets – just go straight. It's on the...north side of Queen. You go by this flower shop, and then you'll see a few buildings with painted doors. One of the doors is blue, then there's a white one, then there's a green door with a picture of a rainbow on it. The door with the rainbow is the one you want. You can just ring the doorbell." He laughed. "Sorry about the directions. I just don't know the names of the streets."

Amazingly, I did manage to find the studio, in spite of Mink's directions, and actually arrived there just as he was unloading an amplifier and bag of cords from his car.

"What you need is a roadie!" I remarked after we had greeted each other.

Mink chuckled. "That's exactly what I need!"

I offered to take the bag but Mink declined, grunting under the burden nonetheless as he guided me up a steep, musty staircase to a surprisingly bright room at the top.

"Wow!" I exclaimed, more because of the colorful wall-hangings than because of the various pieces of electronic technology that were all a mystery to me.

"Here it is," he said, gesturing toward the compact work area by an open window. He walked past me to that area, pulling up a chair for me and then seating himself in a swivel chair in the center of it all. "This is my Mac," he said, flicking on a switch as I sat down. The computer screen came to life.

I looked on, warily. "I've heard all these horror stories about computers, about how you can spend all night working on something and then it doesn't get saved..."

"And the bad news is, those stories are all true," Mink confirmed.

The rumble of traffic reached us from the street below. Here I felt protected, in this haven above it all.

Mink, surveying the computer set-up, appeared concerned for a minute; then he pressed a button and breathed a sigh of relief. I was about to ask him about what he was doing when suddenly a barrage of percussion sounds came from the speakers overhead. It caught me off-guard, but soon the familiar howl of Mink's guitar broke through, and I relaxed in my chair. It was a tune I had never heard before, a funky march with an occasional extra beat stuck in. I pictured a parade of giant reptiles.

Then, just as abruptly as it had begun, it ended. Involuntarily I burst out laughing.

Mink laughed, too. "Wacky, eh?" He turned something off and then settled back, folding his hands across his chest. "So, that's the kind of thing I've been doing on computers."

"Does anyone know that you do this?"

He shrugged. "Ruby knows. The guys in the band know. But the beauty of it is, it's just for me. It's all my own thing. Not that I wouldn't like to do something with it someday. And not that I won't do something with it someday. But right now, it's just for me."

A streetcar clattered past, seeming quiet by comparison.

Mink sat forward, animated by a new idea. As I sat there, he tried playing a particular fragment of the piece, and then altered it, repeating both versions back-to-back until, obviously satisfied, he released a sigh of ecstasy.

I laughed again, and he turned to look at me. "See what I did? I'm just playing the same thing backwards."

I tried to hear it that way, but it only sounded bizarre. I listened some more, finally asking: "How many people do you think will realize that it's the same thing backwards?"

He frowned. "What matters is what it sounds like now. It doesn't matter how it got that way," he replied, and I felt foolish.

The time came for us to leave, Mink to go to a recording session and me to kill time before evening. We collected our things. Mink put his hand on my shoulder and steered me toward the door. "I'll get you a copy of it before you go back to Michigan," he said.

* * *

It was the first time I had been to the Beaches in the summer. All around me people and vehicles rushed past, while only a block away, languid Lake Ontario melted into the sky.

Toting my bag of clothes for the sleep-over, I drifted into and out of gift shops and bookstores, but found nothing of interest there, since I was unable to concentrate on anything but the splendid night ahead. Outside once again in the hazy afternoon sunlight, I walked slowly over to a bench by the lake and sat down, staring out at the water. The lapping of the waves hypnotized me for a while; but I was impatient, and soon found myself on my feet again. There was to be a three-hour interval between my departure from Mink's studio and my arrival at their house to spend the night. The heat had made me dizzy. As I headed back to Queen Street in search of a cold drink, I wondered if Toronto would always be for me a city of wandering, of journeys tortuous and without end.

CHAPTER 11

"Come in Iris! We'll be home soon." The note, in Ruby's round, girlish letters, was printed on a sheet of some pink stationery with cartoon drawings that I had once made for her. It delighted me that she had thought to use it.

With a key Mink had given me that afternoon I went in, set my bags down by the door, took off my shoes, and settled blissfully on the couch.

Once again, I tried to memorize the room, each little knickknack, but there were too many marvelous things: exquisite statuettes, plants hidden in unlikely corners...

It amused me to see the latest issue of *International Musician,* addressed to Mink, on the glass coffee table in front of me. Hard to believe, that the exalted Mink Lasher belonged to the same union as I did. I picked up the union newsletter and leafed through it. As usual, it contained nothing of interest; there was no mention of Mink in the "Canadian Scene" section, although there once had been, when he had toured with Denise d'Angereuse. I noticed a few other papers and letters addressed to Mink in a small pile on the cushion next to me, but with great discipline refrained from looking through them.

Putting down the magazine, I sat in a kind of meditation, trying to infuse myself with the holiness around me, to become worthy of Ruby and Mink, whenever they should arrive.

After what could have been an hour, I heard the outer door being opened and shut. The doorknob rattled, and Ruby came in.

I rose to greet her. "Hi!"

She turned slightly in my direction. "Oh – hi, Iris," she muttered, turning the lock behind her. It crossed my mind that perhaps she had forgotten that I was coming, and might already be forgetting that I was there. Setting down her purse, she hung up her beret in slow motion and lingered by the door, staring off like someone in a trance. Then all at once she recoiled, as if hit by some invisible force. At that point she seemed to remember me. "I'm very tired," she said. "I need to get to bed. Mink won't be home till late."

Dumbfounded, I remained frozen in the middle of the room while she moved past me toward the couch. She threw the pile of Mink's papers aside. "Everywhere I look, I see a mess!" she cried.

I shrunk within myself; this place was so neat compared to my room. I pitied Mink.

Ruby picked up an afghan that had been draped over a nearby chair and flung it onto the couch. "You can use that for a blanket," she directed. Then she paused. "Would you...like something to eat?"

The question sounded nightmarishly surreal, given her mood, but I needed to salvage some bit of this long-awaited occasion. Besides, it was the first sociable thing she had said to me, and I was hungry. "Sure."

She disappeared into the kitchen. I heard her open the refrigerator door. "Do you like peanut butter?" she called to me.

"Yeah, that would be good."

After a minute she reappeared carrying a sandwich on a small plate. She set it down on the coffee table with a clang. "You can just sit there and eat." It struck me as contemptuous somehow, the way she said it.

I knelt down on the floor in front of the table and took a bite of the sandwich. "It's delicious!" I exclaimed. And it was: natural peanut butter, liquidy but rich, between thick slabs of bread made from a medley of unidentifiable grains.

Ruby sat on the edge of a nearby chair, her posture surprisingly stiff and erect, considering this was her own living room. I attributed it to her yoga training.

Neither of us spoke. Suddenly self-conscious about the munching noises I was making, I gulped down the sandwich as quickly as I could.

Outside a car sped past, blaring its stereo down the normally quiet street.

Ruby pulled her sweater about her. "I don't like loud music," she said, shivering. "It repulses me. It ravages the soul."

The implication of her words made me shiver as well, and I began to be very afraid for Mink. The house now seemed full of ominous shadows. My throat contracted, as if Ruby's malevolence had turned the air into something toxic to breathe. I gagged.

"You shouldn't eat so quickly," Ruby scolded, and I hated her for reproving me.

* * *

I had been lying awake for some time when a scratching sound impelled me from the couch. I crossed the room and opened the door to find Zydeco there. He meowed lazily and ambled inside, his fat, tiger-striped body undulating with each step.

Ruby hadn't told me what to do about the cat. I hoped it was all right that I had let him in. Everything had become strange and forbidding; I hesitated to touch anything.

I re-locked the door and went back to lie down again, trying to avoid further trouble.

Before long the cat jumped on top of me and began purring quite loudly, rubbing his face against my hand, which responded to his overtures. He was an unbelievably heavy cat, and I almost couldn't breathe with him there. But he was so warm and friendly that I found him comforting in my anxious state. I squirmed around to get the cat into a slightly more benign position relative to my lungs, and then stroked him as he purred me to sleep.

I was awakened by the clicking of a key in the lock. The cat was gone; it was still night. I closed my eyes again and pretended to be asleep.

A rush of cool air swept though the room. I heard Mink step in quietly, shutting the door with a soft thud. It sounded as if he set something down by the door, perhaps his guitar. His footsteps came lightly across the room until he stood over me.

"Iris," he whispered.

I was stunned, not sure what I should do. Finally, unable to keep up my pretense, I opened my eyes and smiled widely at him. "Hi!" I whispered back.

He grinned, as if pleased that I was awake. "I just got back from a party at Danny Hawks's house," he said in a hushed voice. "It was great!" He took off his baseball cap and set it on a small, covered table, and then ruffled his hair. "I don't want to get `hat-head'!" he laughed.

I sat up, beguiled by Mink's strange exuberance. Surely everything would be all right.

"Danny gave me this suit," he said, pulling the lapel of the gray jacket he had on, which I then noticed for the first time. "He got it for my birthday, but he didn't get a chance to give it to me until now. It's a guitar-playing suit," he went on, striking a mock guitarist pose, hip forward, leg slightly up. He strummed the air with his hand. "DWANG!" he wailed, in imitation of his guitar, and then burst into hysterical though still muffled laughter. It seemed to me that he was either drunk or high, but his spirit had me completely enchanted.

I laughed too. "It looks good on you," I said, uncertain how to react. Then I remembered the cat. "I let Zydeco in. Is that all right?"

"Oh ya. Whatever he wants, do. That's the rule about that. Where is he?"

"He's..." I looked around. "He's by the kitchen."

Mink went over and, stooping down, whisked the giant cat up in his arms. "Fatso-catso-the-pussycat!" he exclaimed, giving Zydeco an affectionate squeeze. Zydeco's legs and tail dangled down, and I noticed that his length measured well over half of Mink's height. With a final squeeze, Mink released the cat.

"I heard a Sunswayers song on the radio yesterday," I said, still in a hushed tone. "I forget which one it was, but it had a teeny-weeny guitar solo."

Mink chuckled wryly. "That's the way it always is with that band. I'm their teeny-weeny guitar player." Our eyes met in tacit solidarity. "Well, I gotta go to bed now," he said. "You'll be here in the morning, won't you?"

I nodded.

"So, I guess I'll see you then. Good night!"

"Good night."

He walked down the hallway and into the bathroom. I heard him urinate into the toilet. It was a robust, luxuriant sound. Never would I have believed that it could be so thrilling to hear a man relieve himself. I stood there for a minute, tingling all over, unable to move.

* * *

The next morning I awoke to a steady rain beating on the bay window and to Ruby and Mink rushing about to get ready for their respective engagements. Mink smiled at me politely and called to Ruby, "I'm gonna start the car." Then he left.

In a few moments Ruby came back into the room. She acknowledged me without enthusiasm as she shoved something into her black handbag and grabbed an umbrella.

"I've got to get going now. This locks behind you," she said, demonstrating the door apparatus for me.

"Bye," I called out, and then sat there by myself, feeling totally drained.

A loud banging on the front door roused me from my brooding. "Iris, open up, it's me!" Ruby yelled.

I rose and let her in.

She shook off her umbrella. "I forgot something," she muttered, hurrying over to the kitchen and taking a booklet from the counter.

"Have a good session," I said in a voice that was supposed to sound cheerful.

"Thanks." With a click and a slam, she was out again.

I took my travel bag into the bathroom and, without washing, dressed myself for my journey home in the rain, realizing then that I didn't have an umbrella.

* * *

"She always trashes him, and she's his *wife!*"

Spoken behind Ruby's back to a bunch of the regulars, the words of the pudgy waitress at Grossman's echoed my sentiments exactly. After all, Mink had always treated Ruby with the utmost affection and kindness, as far as I could tell. I remembered that she had complained about his drinking, but he seemed more charming, if anything, when he was drunk. How could the woman who had won the heart of such an extraordinary man be so disdainful of her good fortune?

"...and she sounds like a cow trying to sing..."

At once I was ashamed of myself for dignifying such spiteful talk with my approval. Ruby had always been like a sister to me, and had been blessed with talent and enlightenment that I could only wish for. Of the two of us, she was by far the more elevated one. If she ever felt displeased with Mink, I knew that she must have her reasons, however incomprehensible they might be to me.

* * *

Mink winced with the intensity of his concentration, the dark furrows in his face reminding me of stripes on a tiger. I was so close to him at the front of the Bamboo stage that at one point he would have whacked me with the neck of his guitar if I hadn't jumped out of the way.

As the song wound down, Sammy, the dreadlocked "preacher" of the band, stepped up to the microphone and, in his thick island accent, bid us all good night.

After the applause ended, the house lights came on, and a generic reggae beat pounded through the club's sound system.

I drifted unsteadily about. It was always so jarring to me when the music ended, but particularly so tonight, this being the last gig before I was to leave Toronto.

Suddenly Mink's arms were around me. "What a girl," he murmured, so softly that I could barely hear it. "What a girl!"

He led me to the side of the stage and we sat down, our legs dangling over the edge.

"So, Iris, I'm gonna miss you when you go back to Michigan. And that's the truth!"

"That's good," I said, and immediately reproached myself for expressing such a selfish sentiment.

But Mink didn't seem offended. "What you have to do," he went on, "is write to me. Write to me every day! I'm terrible at responding, though, so you'll have to say, 'Answer me or I'll kill you!'"

We both laughed. Then Mink drew closer, lowering his tone.

"So, I quit the Sunswayers. This is my last month with them."

That was news to me. "Why?"

"It was too comfortable," he said. I didn't understand, so he elaborated: "I could go on for years like this, just floating along, and it would be easy. But I have other things I want to do, and I can't do them if I have to play with the Sunswayers all the time." His face took on a desperate, yearning expression. "It'll be difficult – I'll be living on the edge for a while, but in the long run I think it's for the best. I hope so, anyway." He slumped over and sighed. "They're looking for another guitarist. Can you imagine what that's like for me? It's like seeing your girl with another guy!"

"He won't be as good as you," I chimed in.

Mink raised an eyebrow. "We'll see."

Soon Sammy came over to talk to Mink. "Hey, mon."

Mink said, "This is my friend Iris."

"I know who she is!"

"She's going away to Michigan, and she thinks we're gonna forget about her," he said, rubbing my shoulder. He smiled at me. "But she'll be back!"

I stood up so that Sammy could have a seat, but lingered for a while, not wanting to leave, ever.

Eventually Mink gave my arm a playful nudge. "Bye, Iris," he said, grinning at me.

It was the last time I saw him before I left Canada.

* * *

When I called to say goodbye, Ruby wished me all the best and told me to visit soon. I asked her about the tape Mink had promised to have completed for me, but she apologized. "He's been sick for a couple of days, and I'm sure he hasn't had time to finish it. But I'll tell him you called."

Peg and Pamela stopped by, bringing me bags of homemade snacks for the trip.

My father came to pick me up, along with his new woman-friend. The overweight blonde secretary helped me with my packing, which I had put off till the last possible minute.

We went out to eat at a Szechuan restaurant in Chinatown before leaving in the crammed rental truck for Ann Arbor.

CHAPTER 12

The fact that I had left Toronto took a while to sink in, but once it did, the desolation was unbearable. Going to clubs in Ann Arbor or around the Detroit area to see bands always ended for me in disappointment, so I avoided that scene. Late at night, alone amid the chaotic clutter of my room at the new co-op, I would listen to the static-filled CBC broadcasts of *Brave New Waves* and *Nightlines,* which featured a lot of Canadian bands I had never heard of. I began to question whether the past four years of my life had ever really existed at all.

* * *

The brown packet that turned up in my mail cubbyhole looked ordinary enough, until I read the return address. Inside, the label on the cassette tape read: "Assorted Mink stuff. Yahoo!"

Scarcely daring to breathe, I carried the holy object to my room and closed the door.

I had expected that Mink's computer music would sound pretty much the same as his guitar solos, except using a computer instead. I was wrong. It amazed me how different these new creations were. Some of them had Latin rhythms, a couple hinted at Bach fugues, one was strident and march-like, and a few would have worked well in the soundtrack to a horror movie.

I played the tape over and over into the night, marveling at the evocative electronic creations, and marveling even more at their creator.

* * *

The next day I called to thank Mink for the tape.

Ruby answered, sounding uncustomarily chipper as she said, "He doesn't live here anymore."

I gasped.

"But let me give you his address and phone number...I know it's around here somewhere..."

It was all I could do not to drop the receiver, I felt so ill.

* * *

The pain didn't let up. It hung over me in everything I did, whether taking a shower or going to class or sitting on the edge of my unmade bed, staring at the floor. Sometimes I would weep all night and wake up with hideous bags under my eyes.

It was simply inconceivable that Ruby and Mink could split up. They were one being. The laws of the universe would not allow that.

I called Mink's new number, getting only his answering machine each time. The voice delivering the recorded message sounded so terse and businesslike that it was hard for me to believe that my inner tumult had anything to do with its owner.

But as the pain continued, and I remembered the nauseating joy in Ruby's voice during the phone call, it dawned on me that perhaps the anguish I was experiencing was not hers but Mink's.

After agonizing over it for days, I sent him a five-page letter, much of it scribbled in the margins, saying essentially that I hoped he was okay.

A couple of weeks later he answered me.

The postcard, bearing a picture of a moose on the front, read:

HI IRIS.
DOING FINE IN TORONTO.
TAKE CARE.

MINK

The card seemed loaded with implications. I had desperately wanted him to write to me; yet now that he had actually done so, it made me uneasy. What was I to make of this? Was he coming on to me? If he were, was that all right? Even to think in such terms must surely be a violation of some sacred principle, although I wasn't certain as to which one. But the thoughts kept pouring in. I studied Mink's card with a scholarly intensity that I had never applied to any of my courses. I needed to know what it meant.

* * *

He had moved in with Eric, the soundman from the Bamboo. I once left a message in which I asked, rather presumptuously, if I could stay overnight at his house on my upcoming trip to Toronto, my first since leaving. "If you don't call me back, I'll show up on your doorstep, and you'll be stuck with me!" I jokingly threatened.

I think it was the only time he returned one of my calls. His cold reaction stunned me. "I'd have to ask Eric," he said in such a way that I immediately knew he wouldn't. "Besides, we're doing some renovations, and there's no room."

I lied and told him I'd stay with some other friends instead. Peg and Pamela had split up – Pamela had moved back to Windsor and Peg, in a radical departure, had gone to elope with a man in his native Finland. Of course, there was Ruby, whose gig was the excuse for my visit. I could possibly have stayed with her but...

After hanging up the phone and moping for a while, I set about booking a room at a hotel.

* * *

Ruby seemed unusually animated as she breezed through her set, bantering with the audience and exchanging quick, enthusiastic words with her bandmembers.

An almost physical ache overwhelmed me. I longed for Mink. His absence wailed though Grossman's like a deafening guitar solo. I choked back tears.

During a break, Ruby came over to me. She put her hand on my shoulder and squeezed it. "Iris, I get the feeling you're not really happy. Is something the matter?"

Did she already know? Regardless, I couldn't tell her. "No, I'm fine," I said, attempting a smile. "You're doing great tonight!"

After suffering through two more sets, I went to bid her good night.

Her aroma of patchouli wafted over me, and I remembered how

much I loved her. "Let's go for a walk," she said.

The crisp night air blew stray snowflakes against our faces as we headed south along Spadina. Occasionally a tacky display of Christmas lights would glare at us from some darkened shop window. Everything was closed and deserted. It felt unsafe to me, but Ruby strolled about as if this were a pleasant morning in the park.

After we had walked a block or so, Ruby drew closer to me. "Iris, I've found someone," she said with a giggle.

"What?"

"I said I've found someone." She said it louder, obviously assuming that the volume of her voice had been the problem. "I have a new boyfriend."

Did she expect me to congratulate her? All I could say was, "Oh."

"His name is David, and he's a luthier," she went on, seeming to savor the word. "L-U-T-H-I-E-R. Do you know what that is? It's someone who makes violins. I spent four days with him last week, and he's the most attractive guy! He slicks back his hair, like this." She tried to show me on herself, but the demonstration was wasted on me. Ruby chattered on: "Iris, he is so eloquent! The beauty of his language...I love being with a man who speaks with such refinement."

We were heading towards Chinatown – me, and this strange woman who resembled Ruby. "I can't believe I'm free again," the woman was saying. "It's like I've had blinders on all these years, and now they're gone, and everywhere I look, there are these gorgeous guys! Did you know that Mink was only my third boyfriend? My third boyfriend! I hardly think I had enough experience to get into a long-term relationship like I did. Now that I'm free, I want to date all the guys I can. It's been ten years – I've proved that I can be monogamous. Now I want to have fun!"

Ruby was practically dancing ahead of me, and I had to hurry to keep up with her. "Mink doesn't know about David yet," she said, starting to pant a little. "I'm going to tell him tomorrow, and it's going to hurt him. I know it will. But I have to tell him. It's over between us. The passion is gone!"

It sickened me to see the woman I had looked up to as a mother-goddess prattling on like a silly schoolgirl. I wanted to defend Mink, un-slicked hair and coarse language and all, but sensed that I would be putting my life in danger if I did so. Instead I asked, "Is Mink seeing any kind of therapist?"

Ruby shrugged. "I don't know what he's doing," she said.

A taxi roared into view. Ruby hailed it for me, hugged me, and sent me on my way. I wondered fleetingly if she would be safe by herself, and then decided, just as fleetingly, that I didn't care.

Slumped in the back of the cab, I felt numb; I felt dead. The streets of an unfamiliar city sped past, galling me with their holiday lights; and suddenly we were there, at the Selby Hotel. In a stupor, I somehow managed to pay the fare and find the way to my room.

Once inside, I curled up on the floor, moaning softly with each breath.

* * *

"She's not a bohemian anymore," Doug said, perhaps bitterly, as we sat together at one of Mink's gigs, discussing Ruby.

According to Doug, she had ditched most of her old friends, so I suppose I should have felt flattered that she was still on speaking terms with me. But I often suspected that she kept up with me for the sheer delight of deprecating Mink to someone who admired him.

"Thank God I'm free of him...it's like being released from Hell..." She was the only one from whom I would have tolerated words against Mink. For, as much as I loved him, I knew that Ruby had done more for him than I ever would. She had practically been his wife, had served him breakfast, had comforted him, had pleased him in every way. She had earned the right to insult him if she chose to.

I learned to avoid bringing up the subject of Mink when talking to her, hard as that was for me, because it was harder to endure her venom. But even if I didn't bring up the subject, she would do it on her own. "Mink used to take me there all the time – how I hated that place!"

Sometimes she would speak of him as "Mink Lasher," as if he

were practically a stranger to her.

Once she referred to him by what must have been some kind of obscenity, for when Tania, who happened to be present, asked with a startled laugh what it was she had called him, Ruby shook her head and wouldn't repeat it.

I wanted to be her friend, but it was so difficult. Ruby had made it clear that she wanted a brand-new identity, and I no longer knew who she was.

* * *

Meanwhile, I would drive up to Toronto every chance I got to catch one of Mink's gigs. When hotel bills became exorbitant, I developed the habit of spending the night in my Ford Ranger, huddled on the front seat beneath sleeping bags and quilts, to doze for a couple of hours before driving back to Michigan for my morning classes. On one occasion, learning upon my arrival that my class had been canceled after all, I immediately got in my car again and headed back to Toronto for another gig that night.

A subscription to *NOW* allowed me to keep up with Mink's performance schedule much as I had before. No longer with the Sunswayers, except for an occasional guest appearance, he was back to his previous existence as sideman to myriad acts: a noisy avante-garde group called brilliantfish, a couple of jazz combos, an actor known simply as Denis who delivered monologues over musical accompaniment, and even Delilah the witch, who performed in full pagan costume with a band of her own.

Even though I drove in from Michigan, I could scarcely count on having so much as two minutes' conversation with Mink. Sometimes he would peck me on the cheek and that would be all; sometimes he would nod to me from the stage; from time to time he would ask if I had had a good trip and might sit and have a drink with me, but more often than not I needed to be content with one or two signs of recognition all night.

Once, inching along the 401 during a blinding snowstorm, I wondered if I would even survive the journey, and if it would matter to Mink either way. Miserably unsure of the answer, I gripped the freezing steering wheel and drove on.

* * *

Then spring came, and there I was, sitting beside Mink in his sports car.

"How's Zydeco?" I asked.

Mink laughed. "Loud. Fat and loud," he answered, speeding up to race through the yellow light nearly a block away.

Only that morning I had been wandering up and down Yonge Street like a vagrant, searching for an excuse to stay in Toronto after Mink's gig the night before. It was one of the few occasions when I had no classes or concerts demanding my prompt return to Michigan, and I had no desire to get back on the westbound highway any sooner than I had to.

It had occurred to me to call Mink at home to see if, just maybe, some last-minute gig had sprung up that had not made it into the pages of *NOW*. The thought terrified me; my years of acquaintance with Mink had done nothing to make him seem any less awesome. Besides, his phone manner was often curt and perfunctory, especially this past year, leaving me to ask myself what I had done wrong. Still, an overpowering need to call him rose within me, and I succumbed.

"Oh, hi, Iris...no, I don't have a gig tonight, but I have some errands to do downtown – things I want to get done before my trip – and you're welcome to come along. I'll swing by and pick you up."

And so it was that I found myself beside him, cruising along in the sleek red Mazda. Light pouring in cast a golden sheen over him, although I doubted that the sunroof alone was responsible. From the stereo Enya's multilayered voice washed over us, complementing the miraculous scene.

"Nice car!" I remarked.

"Ya, I got some dough from going on tour with the Sunswayers. Needless to say, I spent it all. Mostly on this thing," he said, patting the steering wheel.

"Are you going on some other tour? You said you were getting ready for a trip."

Mink squirmed in his seat. “No, I’m going to Mexico. Actually, I’m trying not to think about that.”

It seemed like a good time to change the subject. “So, how is Wally?” I asked.

It pleased me to see him relax again. “Oh, same as ever. Same old Wally. I might be playing with him at the Cameron next month – I’ll let you know.”

Bound to the subway system as I had been as a student, the roads and buildings that sped by us were all brand-new to me. The world out there had a special sheen now that Mink was driving me through it.

My good fortune made me chatty. “I was listening to the Sandalmen album the other day. Does Laird sing with any other bands when he’s in Scotland, or what does he do?”

Mink shook his head. “He doesn’t actually ‘do’ very much. Well, he writes...Basically, he leads a very simple existence.”

Trees arched overhead, somber and rich as Mink’s voice.

Buoyed up by a strange substance that seemed to have replaced ordinary air, I ventured to ask, “Do you ever talk to Ruby anymore?”

“Oh ya. We talk sometimes. We’re still friends.”

I bit my lip and stared out the window. All this time I had wanted Mink to open up to me, to talk to me about his situation with Ruby. Now that he was finally doing so, though, I felt awkward and totally unprepared to deal with it. “I always get depressed when people split up,” I said with effort.

“No, we’re still friends,” he assured me. “It’s not as if we didn’t like each other anymore.” We had turned onto an entrance ramp and were spiraling down to the Don Valley Parkway. “This music sucks,” he muttered, changing the station.

After going to pick up an amp from someone on the north side of town and then heading south again to check out supplies at a new music store, we ended up at a pleasantly air-conditioned Jamaican restaurant.

“I used to come here with the Sunswayers,” Mink told me after we had settled at a table in the middle of the dark, drafty room.

"You still play with them sometimes," I remarked.

"Ah, once in a while. They don't need me very often. I like doing it, though. Especially since Burton's not in the band anymore."

"What's he doing now?"

Mink looked disgusted. "I don't know and I don't care."

A waitress brought us our menus, and with them my first introduction to such terms as "roti" and "jerk chicken." I wanted to ask the waitress to define them for me, but preferred to wait for her to leave and then ask Mink. Most of them he knew, although he was stumped by "chana."

"But you can't go wrong with a roti," he advised me with a grin.

Settling on the potato roti a la carte, I put down my menu. Mink, apparently having already decided, relaxed in his chair, his eyes closed and his head tilted back regally, luxuriating in the breeze from a ceiling fan. At length he opened his eyes again and gave me a faraway smile.

"The food here seems very healthful," I commented.

"Oh, it is." He sat forward. "I've been taking better care of myself lately. I lost ten pounds," he said, spreading his arms so that I could view his new physique. "I've been jogging a lot, and watching what I eat. 'Your body is a temple.' Have you ever heard that expression?"

Of course I had, but it sounded particularly meaningful the way he said it.

Leaning forward even more, he rested his elbows on the table, clasping his hands under his chin. He fixed his eyes on me. "I'm more determined now. I know what I want, and I'm willing to go after it."

A quiver went through me, and I could say nothing.

The waitress came and took our order; then Mink remembered a phone call he had to make. He left the table and I sat there, slightly trembling, compulsively sipping my water.

He returned just as the waitress was bringing our entrees, which were so large as to be decadent.

"You're lucky you didn't decide to get the rice and beans with that," Mink laughed. "You'd never be able to finish it!"

After lunch, Mink drove me back to my car.

"Ciao!" he called to me, beeping twice. Tropical spices still burned deliciously in my mouth as I watched the little red car speed off again, soon to be engulfed in traffic.

* * *

That July my mother and I went on a trip out west. We stayed at a bed and breakfast in Sedona, Arizona. Mystical Sedona, city of crystals and vortices and U.F.O.'s. That's why my eccentric uncle Murray lived there, and that's also what made Sedona the butt of jokes by less imaginative skeptics. Fiery, jewel-hued rocks jutted up to the sky in a million phantasmagorical shapes, only to dissolve into an all-encompassing night. Silent stars hovered in the clear sky, brilliant and omniscient. Anything was possible.

Two nights later, we slept on the edge of the Grand Canyon. It was terrifying – I was certain that we would fall in. The gigantic chasm seemed like a black hole. But in the morning, waking up from a fitful sleep in the car, I witnessed the most spectacular sunrise I had ever seen.

Then California. We coasted along Route 1, which flirted curvaceously with the Pacific. The Hearst castle rose up, far in the distance, on the left. The day was bright and endless. We scanned the whitecaps crashing below us for shapes of sea lions. We didn't see any, but we could have. We could have seen mermaids. Anything was possible. Anything.

In those wild, overblown western landscapes, I dared to make my biggest, most extravagant wish: I wanted to be Mink's wife.

* * *

To be Mink's wife...my dream...

Yet that exalted state lay beyond the scope even of my dreams. It was all I could do to summon up hazy pictures cobbled together from my memories of Ruby and him; and I was certainly no Ruby.

As Mink's wife I would share his bed...

That was by far the most difficult part to imagine. I had, in the course of my life, seen naked men: my father and my brother, very rarely, in person; and others represented in artwork and on film. All this had given me some concept of the male anatomy. But I doubted that Mink would resemble any of these models.

In fact, I doubted that his anatomy was human. Could any human conceive the unearthly sounds that he did on his guitar? My mind conjured up images of him as some sort of serpentine dragon, and I would hardly have been surprised to learn that beneath his clothing he had scales. Although he appeared somewhat small in stature, I attributed to him fantastical powers to uncoil and expand to immense proportions, so huge that I could never envision him in his entirety. Embracing me after many a show, his drenched body, at once cool and hot, had soaked me through my blouse as if with the waters of some primordial lake. I assumed that with marriage I would attain degrees of intuition that would help me satisfy his still unfathomable needs.

To be his wife...if such a creature could truly have a wife, I would be the one.

CHAPTER 13

My love letter went through many drafts before emerging in its final form. By the end of September, the floor of my room at the co-op was littered with shreds of the earlier versions, each one rejected for being too sappy, too wordy, too childish, too whiny, or too boastful. At length I arrived at one that, in my judgment, seemed spontaneous and natural without being ridiculous. In it I told Mink that I knew him better than anyone else in the world and felt that he was my destiny.

Picking out a card with a photo of a flower bouquet on the front, I studiously copied my message word for word from scribblings on the notebook paper. When it was finished, I struggled with myself, resorting to meditation and channeling, until I somehow mustered up enough courage to mail it.

By turns panicked, stoic, and euphoric, I awaited his reply.

* * *

Now, I did expect him to reply.

I knew that it normally took at least a week for mail to get to Canada, so for the first few days after I sent the card I had nothing to worry about. After nearly a week had gone by, however, I grew edgy and often wished I hadn't sent it. Every time the phone rang my heart raced, and sometimes I almost threw up. But it was never Mink, so each time I breathed a sigh of relief.

After two weeks had passed, though, and then three, I grew impatient. Nervous as I was, I ached for him to call, to tell me that he loved me; or, if that was not to be, for him gently to put me out of my misery. He had uncanny powers, limitless wisdom, and he would certainly know the right thing to say.

Maybe he had chosen to write. In that case it would take longer, and I had less reason to be concerned that he had not yet responded. But no letter or card from him ever arrived.

To reassure myself, I would listen to the many tapes and records I had on which Mink had played, either prominently or more subtly in the background. His music had once had a special ability to clear my mind.

Now it seemed to have the opposite effect.

Driving back to the co-op one night after a late rehearsal, I was overcome by anxiety. The unlit road curved away from me, and I felt completely alone.

It had been nearly two months since I had sent Mink my letter. Why hadn't he said anything? How could he leave me in limbo like this? I had trusted him. How could he be so cruel and inhuman? How could anyone? Tears blurred the road in front of me, and I pounded on the steering wheel. "I hate him!" I shrieked. It shocked me, my treachery that I couldn't control.

This didn't make sense. Mink was the most important thing to me, more important than my life. I should just drop this silly pride that was turning me against him and making me such a shrew.

But something new had begun to form inside of me: some fledgling sort of feminine identity. I had never perceived it before, but was acutely aware of its existence now. It had a solid presence that I couldn't push out of the way or ignore. And it demanded an answer.

* * *

Mink had recently joined Danny Hawks, his former bandmate from the Sandalmen, in forming a band called Meander Lane. *NOW* had included a blurb about the band's inception, calling its music a "pleasant blend of folk, rock, and funk, where Hawks's easy-going vocal style contrasts superbly with Lasher's raucous guitar licks." They had done two gigs already, neither of which I had been able to attend because of the university orchestra schedule. However, on November sixteenth, the date for Meander Lane's upcoming show at the Bamboo, my schedule left me free and clear.

* * *

All of the women around Mink looked fantastically gorgeous, like actresses in the old *Star Trek* episodes, who had been filmed through gauze. He introduced me to a neighbor of his, Alicia, a petite, poised blonde with eyes enormous from mascara. She smiled beautifully at me. I felt sick.

Mink soon excused himself to prepare for the set, which was

about to begin. Alicia sat down next to me and proceeded to introduce me to the other two women at the table: her friend Diane, a slender brunette in a strapless gown; and Becky, Diane's sister, who looked like one of the cheerleaders who had tormented me in high school.

The lights dimmed; someone tapped a microphone; then the set began.

The first song faded in from nothing, reaching its full volume as Danny stepped forward. *"If we should pass along the road..."* His fair hair seemed to dissolve into the bright stage lighting as he began to sing.

I ordered a fuzzy navel and, nodding to the music, tried to appear calm.

Mink had a lyrical solo midway through the tune, and I began to relax, to melt into his notes. I was glad to be here, the drive had been good...

The song faded out, to a ripple of applause.

"Thank you all for coming," Danny said, beaming out at the audience. "The next song is one of Mink's, called 'Heaven Weeps.'"

A red beam illuminated Mink as he strummed out a minor-keyed, arpeggiated intro. *'She slipped away from me that night...'"*

The song, so obviously about how Ruby had abandoned him, chilled me to my core. It was good that I had come, to be there for him.

After a couple of songs, Becky announced that she had to go home, but her chair wasn't left empty for long. A woman in a black outfit, wearing a wide-brimmed black hat, sat down. Her face lit up when she saw Alicia and Diane; she removed her hat, and I noticed that she looked rather like Ruby, only taller and with dark hair.

Mink did "Cats and Mice," one of his humorous songs that he had often done with Ruby. After "Cats and Mice," though, there was a problem with the monitors, and the band took a break.

We stood up and stretched. Alicia introduced me to the new woman, whose name was Annette. Annette shook my hand aristocratically.

"Are you a musician?" I asked.

"No, I'm an interior designer," she answered in a soft, low voice.

"Mink and I have been seeing each other for several months."

I don't know what I looked like at that moment; coolly, I went back to my seat. The wound was growing by the second, and I was about to be swallowed by it. Through my most intense glare, I saw Mink squatting down, adjusting something. He appeared the same as ever – the same man in whom I had had absolute trust. I couldn't believe that he would do this to me. He plugged in a cord and turned a knob, intent on what he was doing and oblivious to my fury.

I glared at him through the whole second set. He must have seen it at some point; I thought he looked perplexed for a minute, although he certainly should have expected this.

Mink had screwed up. It didn't matter how masterfully he played, how ingenious the improvisations were that flew from his fingers. In fact, his music seemed more perfect to me that night than it ever had before, reaching into me with an urgent array of bright, magical colors; it didn't matter. His magic was not going to work on me this time. He had wronged me. He had failed.

When the lights came on for the second break, I got up to leave. There was no place for me here, after this...my body moved slowly, unaccustomed to the new set of directions it was being given. It paused near the door. A hockey game was playing soundlessly on the television set above the bar. Players slid absurdly across the ice, my eyes following their antics. I told myself that I would have to go. It all seemed so pathetic, the years I had spent enmeshed in these people's lives. A big mistake. The things I had held most sacred were actually nothing. Somehow I would have to make it out that door to my truck...more than anything I wanted to be back in my truck, moving along the freeway...

As if a voice had whispered in my ear, I heard the words: "CONFRONT HIM."

I hadn't thought of that. And amazingly, it made sense.

I took my seat again, my familiar mindset returning to me. Mink would have an explanation. He would somehow make everything all right, if I only gave him the chance. I had faith.

* * *

After the show Mink came over to our table. "Iris..." he said, eyeing me with what looked like apprehension.

He had obviously felt the bad vibes I had been sending out to him during the second set, but by now I was ready to listen. I wanted him to explain everything to me in a way that I would understand. "Can I talk to you?" I asked.

He shifted his feet. "Not if it's about anything heavy. There was enough heaviness onstage."

It took me a moment to digest his refusal. "Call me sometime," I muttered, picking up my purse and leaving the table. It infuriated me that I had stayed. I had almost left before but had stupidly decided to give Mink another chance. Tables and nameless people whirled around me as I hurried towards the door.

"Iris...don't go away. We'll talk."

Often in times to come, I would wish that I had kept walking, had continued on like a more resolute version of Orpheus, without turning back. But it didn't happen that way.

I turned to see Mink looking straight at me from across the room. Mesmerized by him as always, I headed back in his direction, under the illusion that I had won.

* * *

Putting his arm around my shoulder, he took me to an area to the side of the stage. "What is it, Iris?"

Could it be that he didn't know? That seemed incredible.

When I remained silent, he asked again, with a slight chuckle, "What *is* it?"

As determined as I had been to confront him, I now realized that I had no idea how to do it.

Mink waited, his arm still around me.

In a crackling voice, I began: "Do you read my letters?"

Pressed against him, I felt him laugh as if relieved by my question. "Of course I do! I love your letters."

Frustrated beyond belief, I persisted: "Then you should have told me you had a girlfriend!"

At once he withdrew his arm and took a few steps back. "What are you...Don't do this to me, Iris."

What was *I* doing to *him*? "You should have told me," I went on, my voice getting higher and tighter. "You could have written or called..."

He stared at me. "You couldn't possibly be serious about wanting to be my lover," he whispered.

Staring back at him, I threw myself headlong at the wall of darkness he had erected around himself. "Why not?"

His eyes penetrated me. "You and I will *never* be lovers. With me, what you see is what you get. If you're looking for something more, it just isn't going to happen."

I felt myself begin to evaporate. Mists muffled his attempts to console me; and when he repeated my name as if to summon me back, I barely heard him.

* * *

Michigan felt even stranger than usual. It struck me how much I had before felt Mink's presence hovering about me, silently supporting me through the ordeals of everyday life. He had grown weary of this duty, I told myself. I would have to move on alone.

But I hadn't been alone like that in years, and now, too weak almost to lift a spoon from a bowl of cereal to my mouth, I was certainly in no condition to start.

By the time the next Meander Lane gig came around, I had no strength left.

My truck knew the way. It must have driven me there by itself.

* * *

When I called Mink from a pay phone on Queen Street upon arriving, I got his answering machine. I left a brief message asking him to put my name on the guest list, and assuring him that I would not "do or say anything obnoxious." For some reason it puzzled me that he hadn't answered the phone, and I wondered if he might have killed himself. Shuddering, I pushed the idea from my mind as I hung up the phone.

* * *

Warm lips kissed the back of my neck. "Hi, Iris." Afraid that I would cry again, I didn't dare to look at him.

Mink closed the magazine I had spread out in front of me. "Don't read in here, Iris. It's dark – you'll hurt your eyes."

His unwonted solicitation touched me. I had read in poor lighting at his gigs countless times before, but never had he expressed such concern. As I struggled to reply in some way, he nudged me again. "This is `Solsbury Hill,' by Peter Gabriel," he said, referring to the song being played over the Horseshoe's sound system. I knew that.

Mink took my hand. "C'mon." Suddenly he had me on my feet, one of his arms around my waist, the other raised as his hand clasped mine.

What was he doing? He had already made it quite clear how repugnant to him the idea was of any romantic connection with me. So how was I supposed to respond to this?

"We're dancing," he stated, as though he needed to explain this to me.

Cautioning myself against any physical reaction whatsoever, I avoided his eyes and followed his steps in a stiff, mechanical way.

Soon he gave up and went over to talk to some people at the bar. Baffled, I returned to my seat, certain that I had failed again.

Meander Lane was in top form that night, with Mink and Danny exchanging witty banter between soulful ballads. My anxiety, soon seeming ridiculous amidst such good spirits, began to wane. At the end of the show, after nearly everyone had left, I ventured to approach Mink again.

Beer mug in hand, he sat swinging his legs over the edge of the stage. "By the way, I liked the flowers," he remarked, referring to the bouquet that I had ordered to be delivered to him, along with a note saying that I was sorry.

His easy attitude warmed me, and I knew I was blushing. "What did they look like?" I asked.

He laughed. "They were red!"

He had a close-cropped haircut that gave him the appearance of an ascetic. I noticed that he also had a loop dangling from his left earlobe.

"You got your ear pierced!"

"Ya, I figured, what the heck."

"Did it hurt?" I asked, never having had my own ears pierced.

He shrugged. "Oh, I don't know. I guess it did a bit. Probably still does!"

"Suffering in silence," I chided him.

Mink looked startled for an instant. Then, evidently realizing that I referred only to his earring woes, he visibly relaxed. "Not really. Aaaggh!" he cried in a mock shriek.

We both laughed; then, after gulping down the last of his beer, he stood up. "Well, I gotta get packed up," he announced.

I climbed onto the stage and followed him over to his instrument area. "What was that effect you did, that sounded like you were playing a rubber band?"

"Like I was playing a rubber band," he repeated, making the comparison sound absurd.

"Like, oowah oowah oowah..."

He nodded. "That's the wah wah pedal. Hendrix used that a lot, especially in his song `Voodoo Chile.'"

"I'm not familiar with that one," I remarked.

Mink bent over to disconnect some cords. "That's because you're a young thing," he said. Then he added, very deliberately, "A *young* woman."

That caught me completely off guard. "Okay, I'll see you next time," I mumbled, stepping down from the stage and hurrying away across the dance floor.

"Iris," he called after me.

I reluctantly turned around. Mink had dismounted from the stage and was signaling with his head for me to come back. I sheepishly did so.

He kissed me on the cheek. Waves of his experience and maturity vibrated through me.

After he turned to discuss something with Danny, I stumbled over chairs in my rush to the door.

Tossing about on my car seat that night, I felt as if a wildfire had blazed through my insides, leaving only ashes and scorched twigs in its path.

CHAPTER 14

Back at the co-op, flipping through the next issue of *NOW* that came in the mail, I found an interview with Mink.

A photo of him seated in a contemplative pose with his guitar graced the top of the page. Once I had recovered my breath, I proceeded to read.

Midway through, Mink described an formative experience he had had as a teenager. "I was at a club, and this woman singer at the microphone dedicated a love song to her boyfriend. He was sitting across the room, and as she started singing, he began to cry. It made a big impression on me, that music could have that kind of power to move people," Mink was quoted as saying.

I was touched by his account. As I pondered it, though, my reaction turned sour. Here was Mink Lasher, who obviously possessed such extreme sensitivity as a musician and as a man. Yet for me he felt nothing.

From the photo on the page he gazed past me, unperturbed by my glare.

* * *

Still, I always ended up going back to Toronto.

"Her weekly trek," Mink once remarked while introducing me to a friend at the Cameron. I felt him playfully jab my thigh under the table, but the impact was hard enough to be slightly painful.

In my bulky sweater I felt awkward and unattractive, obviously not his type. When Mink later got up and danced with the buxom waitress, it served to remind me just how far short I fell.

After the lights went on at the gig's end, I remained at my table reading a book, so as not to impose upon Mink right away. When at the end of the chapter I looked up from my reading, none of his equipment remained onstage.

Frantically I looked around. At last I spotted and approached a trimly-dressed, bespectacled Asian man with whom Mink had been speaking during one of the breaks. This was, I had gathered from a few overheard words, Kento (now called "Kent"), the "kid" next door who had gotten him started playing guitar.

"Hello...have you seen Mink?" I asked.

"Mink left a while ago."

My heart sank when I heard that. "He...didn't say goodbye to me! Next time you see him, you tell him that I'm mad at him!"

"Mink is cruel," he said.

Interpreting his comment as sarcasm, I gave a weak laugh.

Kent shook his head. "It's not funny."

Taken aback, I suddenly wanted to defend Mink. "He doesn't mean to be cruel," I insisted.

"You don't have to make excuses for him."

Did this man's glasses give him x-ray vision? For I felt as if he were looking right through me. But I pressed my point: "He may act that way sometimes, but he's so good, he makes up for it."

Kent sneered. "You mean he's a good *guitar player* – he's good *onstage*."

"No! I mean he's a good person!" It surprised me that one of Mink's oldest friends had lost sight of that. Stammering something polite, I hurried away.

* * *

Around Christmas I happened to meet Annette again, this time in the women's washroom at a Bloor Street club called Clinton's. "Hi," I said, greeting her with my friendliest smile to make up for my behavior at our previous encounter.

"Hi, Iris," she said, equally brightly, and it relieved me that she seemed to bear me no ill will.

I saw her at a few other gigs over the next couple of months. Once, at a club in the Beaches called Babbages, she stood near the door talking to Mink, whose back was to me. I couldn't help noticing how her mouth opened and closed in slow motion, reminding me of a fish blowing bubbles. It would have been comical except for the anguished expression on her face.

I never saw her again after that.

Another woman, Leslie, swanlike in a white shawl and gown, was introduced to me at an upscale club on Front Street.

"Iris is great," Mink told her, winking at me. "She puts up posters for me, comes to all my gigs...she's everything a guitar player could possibly want!"

Everything he could possibly want...shaking hands with the new woman across the table, I cringed at how untrue that was.

As more people joined our table I heard her declare to someone, "Mink and I are really, *really* good friends!"

But I never saw her again, either.

"Too bad Mink isn't with Ruby anymore," Devin sighed as I sat across from him at Grossman's.

"Have you met Rachel? She seems nice," I said, referring to Mink's most recent date.

Devin looked away, as if he could see someone I could not in that empty corner. "I miss Mink and Ruby together," he said quietly. "They were a great couple."

* * *

"And there's the magnificent Ruby Treece!" Mink announced into the Babbage's microphone one Friday night.

I turned to see Ruby scurrying toward a table at the rear. My heart surged in my chest when Mink jumped down and dashed across the room to embrace her, and just as quickly dashed back to continue the set.

I went over and sat down next to her, delighted when she squeezed my hand.

"Iris, good to see you!"

A waiter came by, and Ruby ordered a kahlua. We tried shouting into each other's ears to converse, but gave up and waited until the break. How radiant she looked! Had she at last come to her senses and decided to return to Mink? The question burned in my eyes as my lips returned her pleasantries.

Brushing back a loose lock of hair, Ruby laughed merrily. "Men are so dumb!" she said. "Charming but dumb. Women are the smart ones. We're more complicated – we can do two things at the same time. Men are so easily distracted! Any woman can have power over any man just by walking by. You can turn a man's head that easily!"

Even more ashamed of my own ineptitude, I marveled at her confidence. Could it really be so simple for some women?

"And did I tell you? I'm dating Alan – you know, the bass player," she said, nodding towards the right side of the stage.

The sick feeling that I had come to associate with Ruby returned to my stomach, and I had an overwhelming urge to get up and run away from her.

But she scooted her chair closer to mine. "Oh, Iris, I shouldn't even be here," she muttered, her tone suddenly changed. "It's embarrassing! Those guys there – between the two of them, they know just about everything there is to know about me."

In spite of myself, I pitied her in her strange predicament. "You know everything about them, too," I pointed out, not without envy at some of her knowledge.

Ruby laughed. "That's true. I could tell some stories! They probably have more reason to be afraid of me than I have to be afraid of them." She took a sip of her kahlua. "Guys just can't handle breakups. It's pathetic! Mink still hasn't gotten used to the fact that I'm seeing Alan. He'll tease me about it, like, 'Oh, you're going on a date with your boyfriend,'" Ruby said, mocking Mink's deep voice. "It bugs me! Guys are so immature about these things."

The band started up again, and as they played, I tried to discern signs of animosity between Mink and Alan. Subtle gestures, sidelong glances, sneers...try as I might, I saw nothing of the kind. They behaved in a quite friendly and respectful manner towards one another, as far as I could tell.

It frustrated me more than ever how stupid I was, and how much was hidden from me.

* * *

My treks to Toronto became more frequent, if anything, with time. Short of grave illness or a harp performance to which I was already committed on the very night of one of Mink's gigs, there was no obstacle that could prevent me from going.

Fatigue often plagued me behind the wheel when I would drive all night to make it back in time for classes. The tree silhouettes and car lights ahead of me sometimes took on bizarre new forms, becoming jeweled castles or monsters blinding me with their glare. When my car swerved, jerking me to alertness, I would look for a rest stop. There I would grab a coffee or catch a brief sleep from which my travel alarm would jar me awake.

Despite the risks and the extreme discomfort, not to mention the hassle of border crossings, I never regretted a single trip. After all, I had resigned myself to living in two different worlds: in Ann Arbor, one of mind-numbing trivialities and in Toronto, another, truer one of inspiration and freedom. Since the demands of these two worlds were perpetually at odds, it was better to favor the realm of the spirit, as wildly impractical as that might be.

It stung me, though, that I found myself trapped in Ann Arbor for so much of my existence not because my parents or my professors had dragged me here as a captive, but because Mink himself had rejected me. Though I ached to inhabit the better of the two realms on a permanent basis, my failings rendered me unworthy of that high honor.

When the ground hogs returned to our co-op lawn each spring, I would watch them from my window, identifying with the homely creatures doomed to a life of grubbing. They seemed to accept their fate so humbly, and I struggled to accept mine.

CHAPTER 15

"Happy Birthday to You, Happy Birthday to You..." Mink's voice, singing with gusto over the phone, surprised me one August afternoon.

I laughed. "Hi there! My birthday was last week."

"What?"

"It was the fourteenth, but that's okay. This way I get two birthdays!"

"Two birthdays...right. So, how old are ya?" he asked.

"Twenty-seven."

There was silence on the other end. "Twen-tee-se-ven!" Mink finally articulated. "I thought you were younger than that."

"A lot of people do. I guess it's because I'm short."

"Me too. Short people get that a lot."

*A young thing...a young woman...*his words from that night still rang in my ears. Could this new information about my age change his mind?

But Mink startled me out of my ruminations with his next statement: "Anyway, I'm gonna be on T.V."

I think I actually squealed. "You are?"

"Ya, this comedian Alex Everett is hosting a new show on CBC called *Out Tonight,"* Mink explained. "One of my friends is handling the music, and he asked me to audition for the house band. I guess they liked me, 'cause I got the job. The first show is in a couple of weeks, and I think I can get you into the audience. Wanna come?"

* * *

The CBC Building on Front Street looked like a children's toy from the outside – a cube painted with festive red stripes. Inside it was a veritable fortress.

Mink had told me the number to call to get on the audience list, although he had stressed that he would have no time whatsoever to meet with me at any point before the show.

A woman seated behind the desk in the lobby checked my name off her list, and then gave me an orange cardboard pass to which I clung as if my life depended upon it. I waited about an hour, taking my place in a long line, until groups of us were escorted by elevator to the studio.

Seating in the audience was not guaranteed, and it looked for a long while as if some of us would have to watch the show on the giant T.V. screen in the CBC lounge. Fortunately, there did turn out to be enough room, and at last I was pointed to a seat near the back of the studio.

On a small platform to one side of the stage, the house band sat at their instruments, joking amongst themselves. Mink, in an embroidered cloth hat but otherwise clad simply in black, arranged some sheet music on his stand. I had never before seen him use a music stand. Once he shaded his eyes with his hand and seemed to scan the audience. I waved, but he showed no indication of having seen me.

Soon the house lights dimmed and the stage lights came on. I kept my focus on Mink as he and the band blasted out the theme music; and afterwards, throughout the show, when they struck up before and after station breaks; and even when they sat idly in near darkness, as they did most of the time, supporting the host and his guests with applause and periodic hoots of laughter.

* * *

"Where were you after the show?" Mink reproached me the next time I called. "I came out again to get my guitar, and you had already left."

"I...didn't know you were coming back," I stammered.

The truth was that he had been so adamant that he would have no opportunity to meet with me that I had hurried away afterwards for fear of being a nuisance. It heartened me that I had apparently misunderstood.

"You were great!" I gushed.

"Come back anytime. I told Glenda at the desk to let you in whenever you show up."

* * *

I did go whenever I could. Many of my weekends, though, had already been booked up with rehearsals and concerts. If I couldn't be there in person, I would watch the program in my room as it aired, or would tape it for later.

Seeing Mink on T.V. week after week, with close-ups of him beaming, jumping, wreaking havoc on his guitar – it should have been a dream come true. Yet when he would come on the screen, it was not a pleasant sensation that I experienced.

This was not Grossman's or the Bamboo or any of the familiar venues where I had so often heard him play. I had not bought a ticket; I could not support the band by ordering a drink; there was no need for me to put up posters; no need for me to clap or cheer; no need for me even to be there. On my T.V. screen I saw the same view seen by thousands of other people across the United States and Canada.

Furthermore, "The Music," as the house band had been dubbed, was not a group that I knew personally or had bonded with in the clubs. It stung me that this band rather than any of the others should become the vehicle of Mink's success. All these years I had considered him "my guitarist," but now it turned out that I had no more claim to him than the next person. Completely aware of the pettiness of my emotional state, I nonetheless couldn't help it. My old anger would rise up in torrents, and I struggled to keep it down.

* * *

Following the last show in December, Mink invited me, along with a few of his friends who had turned up that night, to a CBC Christmas party at a fancy club in the Skydome.

His friends all began to mingle right away, and since Mink had, as usual, turned into a party animal, I found myself sitting alone, sipping a glass of ice water.

Across the room, Mink and the host were loudly engaging in horseplay. Mink threw his arms around Alex and showered his face with kisses.

"Fuck off, Mink!" Alex protested.

Mink ignored him and continued, nearly pulling Alex to the floor.

"Fuck off, Mink!"

Eventually Mink released him. Alex brushed himself off and two of them resumed conversing with the other partyers in the vicinity.

Somewhere in the midst of their camaraderie, I happened to catch Mink's eye. He merely looked away and carried on with his socializing.

Crestfallen, I sat there, chewing on ice cubes.

Canned dance music blared through the club, with the bass turned up so loud that I could only occasionally recognize the songs. A waitress brought around small dishes of sherbet and I took one, afterwards fiddling like a two-year-old with the long spoon.

Warm fingers caressed my neck, continuing through my sweater all the way down my back. "Hey, babe."

Surging up, I dropped my spoon onto the floor.

"I loved your tape," he said, referring to the crude recording that I had recently made for him of my poetry set to improvisations on the harp. Over the clamor of the room, I heard him whisper to me: "You're a GEE-NEE-US." Massaging their warmth into me, his hands dispelled all my hurt and doubt.

* * *

Driving home that night, with a sly sax tune coming over the radio, I knew I had to do something, something daring and spectacular, to express what was inside me. Mink was the ultimate, the alpha and the omega. I had to do something.

* * *

I got a tattoo. It was something that had been in the back of my mind for a while – my friend Shelley had talked about getting one, perhaps a rose or a butterfly. And I had seen on an afternoon talk show how a fan of Dolly Parton had tattooed his body in seven places to prove the depth of his devotion to her. So, to me, it presented itself as the obvious thing to do.

The tattoo artist at a local parlor helped me with the design: a fiery red-and-orange guitar surrounded by stars and superimposed with "Mink Lasher" in jagged letters.

As she traced the black outline with her needle I cringed; the coloring felt comfortable by comparison.

When I removed the bandage and saw the fresh, raw work of art on my arm, I knew that I had at last become beautiful.

* * *

Mink gasped. "That's not real, is it?" he shouted. Then, as if trying in vain to reassure himself, he muttered, "You wouldn't do that. Tell me you wouldn't do that. That thing can't be real!"

I hadn't known what sort of reaction to expect, but I hadn't expected this.

Against the CBC marquee he stood in dark silhouette above me. "Iris, that tattoo isn't real, is it?" he asked me again.

"Yup," I said with a sheepish grin.

He took a step back from me on the snowy sidewalk. "Sometimes you scare me," he said, and then repeated, "Sometimes you scare me."

The wind felt particularly chilly right then, whipping capriciously out of nowhere, and stopping just as abruptly.

"That's almost like going too far," Mink continued. "Almost like crossing the line."

"Almost, but not quite?" I asked hopefully.

Mink appeared to be in no mood for joking. "That's – that's my whole name! That's ME!"

It felt as if a giant weight were crushing me into the pavement. I wanted to retaliate, to yell back at him that Ruby had told me "Mink" wasn't even his real name. But I couldn't speak to save my life.

"Iris...don't get like that..."

Chatty people arrived by cab, scurrying past us to the door.

"Almost, but not quite. That's right," Mink affirmed in a lame attempt to cheer me up.

I was about to cry. I couldn't do that right now.

"Kiss me!" he pleaded.

I stood frozen, like some absurd fixture projecting up from the sidewalk. Numbly, I became aware of him pressing me into the building, where he made idle, one-sided conversation for a few minutes before going up to rehearse. In the lobby, I waited without enthusiasm for the elevator to take me upstairs.

* * *

The Music's seven bandmembers came down the hall, singing their parts, in parody of the theme music. Mink caught sight of me. "You caught us practicing," he laughed; then he came closer. "You haven't been crying, have you, you scandalous thing?"

It was impossible to deny. I could feel how red and puffy my eyes were, how my nose was all stuffed up, how tears had hardened on my cheeks. "Are you mad at me?" I asked in a quivering voice.

"No." He was very close to me now, inches from my face. "If I were mad at you, I would tell you."

I couldn't control my sobbing. The place seemed to be shaking around me.

It was Mink who was shaking me. "Tell me you believe me!" he demanded.

I was incapable of telling him anything.

"Tell me you believe me or I'll kill myself! I'll jump out that window right now, unless you tell me you believe me!"

I almost thought he would. Even as I stood there in my hysteria, which seemed to be rubbing off onto him, I realized that this was not something with which he ought to concern himself right before appearing on national television. Yet I stood there in my devastation, a blubbering idiot.

"Okay, I'm...honored," he said, trying another tack. "It's like a kind of...gift." The expression on his face, though, was one of horror, as if he beheld some monstrosity. "I'm honored. But you can't expect me to feel too honored!"

"W-why not?" I stammered.

He gave me a look of utter dismay, as if I were beyond all reason, before going to join his bandmates in the studio.

I lingered in the hallway as long as I could. Then I assumed a position virtually under the audience risers, where shadows hid my face.

* * *

The show went off without a hitch. Mink played spectacularly, as always. He was the consummate performer. Nothing fazed him once he had a guitar in his hands. As he passed by me a couple of times between band numbers, I felt something I had never experienced before: dislike for him. For the first time since I had met him, I could see him as someone entirely separate from me. What a big shot he was, strutting around in his cowboy boots and hat, with his blaring guitar riffs drowning out everything else. Such a poseur!

But after the show, when Mink came over to me again, my knees weakened and I thought I would collapse.

"Where is that thing?" he asked. Taking my arm and rolling up the sleeve, he kissed my tattoo. Then he was gone.

Before I dragged myself from the studio, I couldn't help pausing to stare at the band area where Mink might reappear. Eventually he did – with a woman in a pale blue gown, luminous as an angel, who stood on tiptoe to kiss him.

That night, huddled under my sleeping bag on the front seat of my Ranger, I wailed myself hoarse. Any passerby would surely have thought that I was being brutalized in my truck.

* * *

So I was a monster to Mink. I scared him. Looking at my own flesh, I imagined it covered with slime. Such a repulsive creature I must be!

Next Friday was the final taping of the show, but I would spare Mink my odious presence. I owed him that.

* * *

"Where were you on Friday?" he asked, when I finally broke down and called him.

"I had...I had a rehearsal for an orchestra concert."

"I thought you'd be there. We all had a party after the show. I was hoping you'd come."

Upon hearing those words, I nearly kissed the phone, so relieved was I that my self-imposed exile could at last come to an end.

* * *

While *Out Tonight* was renewed for another season, it

underwent major revisions that included replacing the band. In truth, there had been several scathing reviews, a couple of which singled out The Music for ridicule. “Nauseatingly exuberant,” read one review, in a blatant jab at Mink, by far the liveliest bandmember. “Think there’s nothing more annoying than television jingles? You obviously haven’t heard Everett’s band, The Music,” quipped the other.

I was devastated when I heard the news.

“Those things always happen in T.V.,” Mink said as he walked me back to my car after a Meander Lane gig.

I was amazed at his philosophical outlook.

“The show was getting lousy ratings, so they had to change it,” he went on. The long Queen Street block stretched out ahead of us. “So where is your car, anyway?”

“Probably about a half mile away,” I said with an embarrassed chuckle.

“A *half mile?”* he exclaimed. “Forget it – I can’t walk a half mile. There are cops out. And look at me,” he laughed, spreading out his arms in mock display, “I’m *wasted!*”

I smiled. “That’s okay. I can get there by myself.”

He draped his arms around me in a loose hug, and then I proceeded on my own.

* * *

A new feature had been added to my Toronto ritual: even in hot weather, I needed to wear long sleeves. Mink hadn’t specifically told me to, but the tattoo had obviously disturbed him so much that I felt it would be easiest just to keep it covered at all times in his presence. Inwardly I prayed that he would at some point take pity on me, especially in the summer.

Once, as I sat perspiring in Grossman’s, Mink asked, “Aren’t you hot?”

Looking away, I replied that I liked hot weather. And he left it at that.

CHAPTER 16

Since being severed from *Out Tonight,* Mink had gone back to his usual assortment of club gigs, although Loudest Rain seemed to have fizzled out, everyone having become too busy with other projects. Most of Mink's energy now seemed to go into Meander Lane, which had been dormant for the past several months.

I saw Meander Lane at a venue called C'est What?, which occupied the basement level of a building on Church Street.

Going up to the stage to talk to Mink after the show, I waited behind what appeared to be a couple of his old friends, neither of whom I had ever seen. Mink hugged the middle-aged woman and then energetically shook her male partner's hand.

"That was some very passionate playing tonight," said the woman, her eyes aglow.

Mink bowed his head.

"You're so devoted to your music," she observed.

"It's my life," he affirmed. I felt both admiration and sadness at this; it made him so remote, so far beyond my reach.

When my turn came at last, he suddenly looked distracted. "Fuck, I have to give Pete directions..." He climbed back up onto the stage, leaving me somewhat vexed and unsure what to do.

Of course, I waited. After Mink had finished talking to his drummer, he went over to the bar and sat there for a while, drinking from a mug of beer.

When I approached him, he started and then laughed. "Have a seat," he said, pulling out a stool for me.

I sat down. "Great gig!" I chirped.

"Ya, it wasn't bad." He rubbed one of his shoulders. "I'm a bit sore from it, though. And then I have to meet with Danny tomorrow – oh, did I tell you? We're going in to do some recording."

He hadn't told me. "You're doing a Meander Lane album?"

"That's the idea. We worked out a deal with Bill – he's the guy who runs the studio where we did the Sandalmen album. He's letting us do the recording on spec."

"What does that mean?" I asked.

"'Spec' – you know, like 'speculation.' It means we don't pay now, but if the album hits it big, then Bill gets a cut."

"Of course it'll hit it big!"

Mink, still rubbing his shoulder, managed a grin.

"Which songs are you doing?" I knew all of them by heart.

"We're still trying to decide that. One of 'em, though, is gonna be 'Heaven Weeps.' Then he gave me a significant look. "Do you want to play on that tune? I was thinking about that yesterday. It's about angels, so a harp might go well in it. In that bridge part," and he sang with almost comical sincerity: *"Angel love, angel light, shine on me tonight..."*

My head swam. "Yeah...I'd love to!"

"I'll have to talk to Danny about it first...call me and I'll let ya know."

* * *

Billion Sound, on the northern edge of Toronto, lay hidden on a sidestreet, behind car dealerships and strip malls. Elated at finding it for the first time, I set down my quilt-covered folk harp and knocked triumphantly on the locked door. Muffled barking reached me through the glass as a fat cocker spaniel tried its best to ward me off.

Eventually Danny appeared and, gently brushing the dog aside, let me in.

"Is this the right place?" I asked in jest.

"Heck, no!" he laughed as he escorted me down a winding hallway.

In the wood-paneled studio, Mink and a lanky young Native Canadian man with braids were discussing something at the control panel. After a few minutes, Mink grimaced and sank into a black couch at the back of the room. "Ya, whatever," he sighed.

Danny, who had gone into the recording chamber to tune his guitar, came back out and introduced me to Jason, the sound engineer.

"And that lump over there on the couch," Danny remarked, with an expansive gesture of his arm, "is Mink."

"Hi, Iris," Mink muttered without opening his eyes.

Recalling the grueling nature of Mink and Ruby's recording session of years ago, I felt an increasing sense of dread at my own upcoming attempt at the microphone.

"Have a seat," Jason said in a nasal baritone, making adjustments with some knobs all the while.

As I hesitantly approached the couch, Mink got up and began to pace. "Jason, could you be a good lad and solo the bass track for me?" he asked, recovering some of his sense of humor.

When Danny informed me that it would be a while before they got to my part, I was immensely relieved.

From my black-cushioned spot, I watched the goings-on of that morning with rapt attention. The musical proceedings, as with the session on Phoebe Street, baffled me – how the players would fret and debate over various takes that sounded virtually identical to me; and how improvisations that amazed me would be met with friendly derision by Mink and Danny. It often seemed to me that the god of true artists must be some insatiable deity, ravenously devouring the energies of all who worshiped at the altar, and always needing more.

At one point Phil, the keyboard player, seemed to have had enough.

"Well, it's easy for you guys to sit there and criticize..." he blurted out.

Mink turned to Danny. "Aw, what's he yammering about?" he asked, suppressing a yawn.

"Yammer, yammer," Danny chimed.

I, meanwhile, had begun to be alarmed, but Phil soon relaxed and did another take that was more to their liking. All good will apparently restored, I, too, relaxed, savoring the experience of being there. Mink sat in front of me on a swivel chair by the control panel, and I loved watching the soft folds of skin in back of his neck, visible with his new haircut that left his head covered with fuzz.

After Phil had finished his part, and Danny had laid down an acoustic guitar track, we took a break for lunch in the studio's fluorescent kitchen. An obese man with a gray beard was already seated at the round table, feeding scraps of his sandwich to the cocker spaniel.

"Hey, Bill!" Mink greeted him with a hearty slap on the shoulder.

Bill, Danny informed me during our introduction, owned the studio. "He's the 'Bill' in 'Billion Sound'!"

As the large man rose to shake my hand, Mink came beside me. "This is Iris, our biggest fan," he said.

"Our *only* fan!" Danny added with a chuckle.

I smiled and shook Bill's meaty hand.

A lunch of cold cuts commenced, during which most of the conversation, about mutual musician acquaintances and newly-purchased recording equipment, went over my head. The cocker spaniel, who turned out to be called Paisley, piteously howled up at the table until Bill chased her away.

One of the bass tracks needed to be re-done, and the afternoon session consisted mainly of deliberations among Mink, Danny and Paul, the bass player, as to what sort of "feel" the bass line should have.

As four o'clock approached, Mink sat down next to me. "Iris, how long are you in town for?" he asked, as I moved over to the next cushion to make room for him.

"Till Friday." Cleo, my friend from the University of Toronto, had kindly agreed to put me up in her basement apartment for the next few days.

"Good. I don't think we'll have time to get to your harp thing today..."

"That's okay," I replied, again relieved. "It'll give me more time to practice."

* * *

They didn't get to my part the next day, either. Mink had gotten a call for a jingle session that afternoon, so he left early, having arrived an hour and a half late that morning. Danny did some vocals, which sounded fine to me, although he severely rebuked himself for "rotten" intonation.

Wednesday I was astounded to see Ruby enter the room. I rose to meet her and she gave a limp smile, but soon slipped back into the hall, followed by Mink.

Danny laughed. "That Ruby – gotta love her!"

"Is she singing on this tune?" Jason grumbled, without looking up from his board.

My heart raced. It had been ages since I had heard Ruby sing.

But it ended up being a mysterious process. Mink came back into the studio and ordered everyone out except for Jason. The rest of us – Danny, Phil, and myself – drifted into the kitchen, Danny and Phil joking about feeling jilted; to me it was no joke. An hour or so later Mink and Ruby emerged again, both looking extremely worn-out.

Ruby's vocals, as I heard in a later play-back, were barely audible, even subliminal, adding the slightest shimmer to a background vocal line that Mink had previously laid down.

* * *

"Well, I'm gonna go get some beer," Mink announced midway through the next day's session. He grabbed his jacket and, turning to me, asked, "Wanna come?"

The question may as well have been rhetorical; he must have known I would follow.

A drizzle greeted us as we left the building for the first time since morning. It had rained quite heavily before, and gray clouds still hung almost tangibly above us.

"'Heaven Weeps' sounds really good," I said, practically skipping along the shiny, wet pavement as we walked down the block to the store.

Mink coughed, clearing his throat. "That song is always weird for me, even though it's one of my oldest ones. I wrote it when my mother died."

So it wasn't about Ruby leaving him, as I had supposed. This intrigued me, and I began to reconsider the song in this new light. After a few minutes I asked him, "What was your mother like?"

He didn't answer right away, and we continued to pick our way around little puddles that had formed in broken parts of the sidewalk. "I think she was confused by it all," he said finally.

I waited for him to say more, but heard only our footsteps on the pavement. "'Heaven Weeps' is probably my favorite Meander Lane song," I mused.

A car whizzed by, splattering us with mud. "Careful," Mink said, pulling me away from the road, "or *you'll* be weeping!"

* * *

"He really should let Danny do all the songwriting for Meander Lane," said my passenger, Caplan, as we cruised along in the rural darkness of Highway 404. "Mink spills out his guts in his songs. So what you get is honesty. But honesty doesn't necessarily make great art."

Gritting my teeth, I said nothing.

We were on our way to Newmarket, where Mink had a gig with an R&B band called Redder Soul. I hadn't known of it until near the end of the recording session, when he had asked if I could give his friend a lift there.

Caplan, a lanky architectural draftsman, smelled faintly of cologne. Even though his comments about Meander Lane grated on my nerves, I was glad to have him there, navigating us through this murky region just north of Toronto where, in all my journeys, I had never been. He could guide me to Mink.

* * *

Still carrying one of the bottles of beer that Caplan had bought for me during the first set, I stood chatting with Mink in the hallway outside the washrooms.

I chuckled. "It's funny – I can drink three grasshoppers pretty quickly and not notice it much. But this is my second beer, and already I'm so dizzy I can barely stand up!"

Mink held his Molson Export bottle forward as if to illustrate something. "It's because beer goes all through your body. It fills you up." He grinned. "Ya, every drink has its own kind of buzz."

Hazy images of his wide-ranging experiences whirled though my brain. "Can you...turn around for a minute?" I asked him.

He looked puzzled but complied with my request.

I reached out an unsteady hand and began to stroke the back of his neck. It felt rather awkward, since I wasn't used to doing this sort of thing, but I tried to be sensitive with my fingers as they moved over his moist skin. After several seconds I stopped, satisfied that I had accomplished my goal.

Mink turned to face me again. "What did you do?" he asked.

I hadn't expected that the act would require an explanation, but I told him, "When we were in the studio, I kept looking at your neck, and I always wanted to do that."

"Oh." Then, to my absolute mortification, he began to rub his skin where I had just stroked him, rubbing it hard, as if to get my germs off his body. "Well, I gotta go tune up," he said, leaving me in the hallway as he walked off towards the main room, still rubbing the back of his neck.

* * *

Friday arrived. I had gotten apprehensive – they seemed to be in no hurry to get to the harp part, even though this was to be my last day there. Still, I had resolved not to complain, even if it meant they would record me at a future session instead – or not at all. I had to be stoic...

"Irisinia!" A hand ruffled my hair.

Looking up at Mink, I laughed.

"So this is harp day, ain't it?" He had read my mind.

"Yup!"

He sank onto the couch cushion next to me with a dramatic sigh. "A whole week of Meander Lane, it's enough to drive anyone nuts."

"Not me! I like it."

Mink lighted a joint and held it out to me but I declined, as always. He took a long drag and then exhaled. "You don't do pot, you don't smoke...If it weren't for the grasshopper things you drink, I'd say you were one of those purists."

Remembering the aversion he had for purists in music, I forced an uncertain smile.

"That's cool, though," he said. "Everyone's different."

Relieved, I asked him: "Why do so many musicians use marijuana?"

In a hushed, almost reverent voice, he said: "Marijuana is *very* good for music. A lot of drugs aren't. Cocaine isn't. Heroine isn't. But I think marijuana is one of the best things for music. That's how I learned to play the guitar, by smoking marijuana. The trick is to get just the right amount, so that you control it and it doesn't control you. Try it sometime. You'll hear things you've never heard before."

It left me unconvinced – here the greatest musician I knew was divulging to me the secret of his genius, and this unsavory substance was it? I couldn't accept that. For I had known other people who smoked marijuana, but no one else like him.

* * *

That afternoon I found myself isolated in the studio booth, headphones on, seated at my harp.

A sudden panic gripped me. All the other people Mink and Danny had recruited to do parts on their album had been called upon for their excellent playing. But here I was, some weird, freakish thing, in this room only because of my bizarre obsession with Mink. Surely they must be ridiculing me out there...

Jason's voice came through the headphones. "Okay, Iris, just play along with the track for a minute so we can get some levels."

As the song came on, I began to pluck, softly picking out the melody and a basic accompaniment, unsure how to ornament it, despite having tried out a few ideas in my practicing.

I heard Mink's voice in the headphones. "Iris, that was good, what you just did. Do it again."

A surge of confidence went through me. When the same music came on again, I repeated what I had just done.

Mink's voice spoke to me again. "You're nervous and you're rushing a bit. Relax and play it a little slower."

My heart was pounding insanely. Maybe Mink could even hear it out there. I took a few deep breaths and tried again.

After two or three more efforts, the music in the headphones ceased. Amidst background noises from the room, Jason's voice came on and asked, "Would you like to hear that?"

Emerging from the booth was like re-awakening from a sound sleep. All around me came cheers and slangy utterances of praise from the guys in the band.

As Danny pulled up a chair for me, Jason fiddled at the control board and then settled back.

Through the overhead speakers came the part I had just played, although it sounded much bigger and richer than it had when I had sat at my harp and picked it out.

After the short section was finished, Jason turned around and asked me: "So, are you happy with it?"

I had actually heard a couple of glitches, but if it met with their approval, I certainly wasn't going to say anything. "I guess."

So that was that.

* * *

A few months later I had the privilege of sitting in on some of the sessions at a downtown studio where Mink and Danny were mixing the tunes. "Heaven Weeps" took up two consecutive nights.

Long after midnight of the second session, Danny sat at the mixing board beside Vaughan, a sandy-haired British Canadian who, I had been told, had worked with the likes of Joni Mitchell and Buffy Sainte-Marie.

Mink paced about the room, rubbing his eyes. "Let's hear that again..."

Caffeine pills and beer had upset my stomach badly. My head ached as well from lack of sleep. Doubled over in a chair in the back of the room, I focused on the men's discussion with all my remaining powers of concentration. When my solo came on, I heard Mink ask, "Do you think the harp is too loud?"

"No, it sounds good," Vaughan answered.

"Okay, but maybe something else should be louder. Maybe the

harp isn't that important. Should we boost the vocals, perhaps?"

"No, it sounds good to me..."

With one hand I pressed into my stomach, and with the other I covered my mouth to muffle the groaning.

* * *

Meander Lane had indeed worked out a special arrangement with Billion Sound, and with Vaughan as well. But whatever it was that they had negotiated, it didn't begin to pay for the amount of time required by musicians as exacting as Danny and Mink.

Although they never asked me for money, they appeared to have no other source; and I believed that they would have sat and waited for money to rain down from the sky rather than put out a product that fell short of their standards. This was, after all, no teenaged garage band – these were some of the finest musicians in the world, and they deserved a chance to create an album worthy of themselves.

I found that I was eligible for student loans, in addition to the money my father still gave me. Also, I was continually being barraged with credit card applications.

Before long I had eight credit cards. And Meander Lane would have their album.

CHAPTER 17

Danny bustled with good humor as he set a large cardboard box on the table. After grunting from the effort, he turned to me with a bright smile. "Well, here they are!"

I drew closer and peered into the box. Stacks of compact discs, entitled "Upside Up," sporting one of the band's old photos gleamed in the light of Danny's kitchen.

"Well, it's about time!" I exclaimed.

"You could say that," he agreed.

The CD had been over a year in the making – or much longer, if one counted the composition and development of the songs themselves. Danny had asked me if I would be willing to send out a few copies to radio stations in the States, and I had gladly accepted the job.

By now I was quite fond of Danny, who seemed to have only this one aspect to his personality, sunny as his head of golden curls.

As he poured tea for the two of us, I felt an overpowering urge to open up to him. "Does Mink ever...hurt your feelings?" I asked, astonished at my own indiscretion.

To my surprise, Danny chuckled. "Mink is *brutal!* He says things without any tact, just whatever comes into his mind. He can't help it. It's the way he is." Then he looked at me, his smile changing to an expression of concern. "Did he say something that hurt you?"

"Oh, I don't know..." Struggling with myself, I fell mute.

Danny, in a quiet tone, went on: "You see, in him, the dark side is very strong. If he hadn't gotten into playing the guitar, he probably would have killed himself or done himself in with drugs."

"God..." I hadn't known that.

"I worry about him," Danny continued. "He's such a lone wolf. I mean, he's had girlfriends, but he always compares it to how it was with Ruby, so he's never happy. I pray for him, I do."

Sitting here talking to Danny about him, I felt closer to Mink than I ever had.

The boxes of CD's lay before us like some miraculous treasure.

"How are you going to get a record deal?" I asked, unsatisfied with the vague answers Mink had given me a couple of times to the same question.

Danny flashed a wide grin. "Oh, don't you worry about that. We have connections in management."

* * *

They had no connections in management. Or, what connections they thought they had had fizzled out, either – unbelievably – not impressed by "Upside Up," or, for whatever other reason, not willing to help the band.

It ended up with my taking more of the CD's back to Michigan with me, to see if I might have better luck sending them out in the States.

* * *

Someone whistled. I turned to see Caplan waving his arms above his head to signal me. Glad to see a familiar face at the Bamboo, I went over and sat down at his table.

"Iris, meet Lisa," he said, introducing me to a slim, dark-complected woman seated to his right. "She's Mink's girlfriend."

I reached over and shook hands with her, and the three of us began a sporadic conversation. I learned that Lisa had come over from Trinidad several years before and now worked as a florist. Although polite, she looked somewhat sour or bored, but would perk up whenever Mink came by.

"Lisa, Lisa!" Once he scooped her up in his arms and kissed her; another time he sat down beside her and clasped her hand, murmuring apologies for his busy schedule. Both visits were short, and neither time did he appear to notice me.

* * *

When I approached Mink after the show, he whipped around with a frantic glare. "*Go take Lisa upstairs!*" he demanded. Then he rushed onto the stage to tend to his equipment.

Meekly, I complied. After I had led her up the stairs to the room Mink had shown me before, cluttered as always with boxes and beer bottles but eerily empty of other people, we sat on the torn couch and tried to chat. I told her about my trip up from Michigan, and the long delay at the border.

"You drove all the way up here to see him?" She seemed incredulous and a bit wary.

"Yeah, I do that sometimes," I said, brushing it off. I noticed that she was rubbing her neck a little and asked her if it hurt. I was surprised to learn that it had recently been broken in a car accident and was almost all healed.

"My mother told me that, when you're sick, you should never stay in bed. The bed takes your strength. If you don't use your muscles, you will lose them. So even though the doctors told me to rest, and told me not to move my neck, I would move it..." She shook her head vigorously from side to side to demonstrate. "And it got better!"

"That's amazing," I said.

She was sniffling. I knew she didn't have a cold, because I was sniffling, too, for the same reason: I was trying not to cry and not really succeeding. Mink had made it clear that he wanted to be rid of us, he had sent us upstairs...

All the while I was painfully conscious of my two scabbed boils on opposite cheekbones, as if put there for some perverse kind of cosmetic adornment.

"Where are his guitar strings?" Lisa suddenly asked me.

"I don't know," I mumbled, adding inwardly: and I don't care.

She rummaged through his bags, and actually managed to find them. As I sat there, purposefully idle, she curled up the strings and put them back in their wax paper envelopes. This was something I had never thought of doing for Mink, since I hesitated even to touch his equipment for fear of damaging it. At the moment, though, I didn't want to help him in any way whatsoever, and was disgusted that poor Lisa did.

We heard footsteps coming up the stairs.

Lisa lit up. "It's Mink! He always makes that sound," and she made a guttural noise, almost a belch, in imitation. I had never noticed before that Mink did that. It irked me that she had noticed something about him that I had missed.

"Irissaleesa," Mink crooned, blending our names, as he entered.

It melted me to see him so cheerful, at last. Lisa and I both beamed – our savior had come. "It's about time!" I exclaimed.

That comment marked the end of our short-lived happiness.

"I'm working!" Mink blasted.

There was a stunned silence. Finally I said, "I was just kidding!"

Mink pulled up a chair next to us. "Ya, but you touched a nerve." Then he addressed Lisa, taking hold of one of her hands and caressing it. "I feel terrible that I haven't been able to spend more time more time with you. I mean, you come all the way here from Hamilton and I just say, 'Go upstairs and talk to Iris...'"

That stung me. He had asked me to entertain his girlfriend, and I had done my best under the circumstances; now he spoke about me as if I were something miserable to get stuck with... "We were having a fine time without you," I cut in.

Mink laughed uneasily. "Thanks a lot," he muttered back.

After more apologies to Lisa, we went back downstairs, Lisa and me carrying the lighter bags as we all loaded Mink's equipment into her car. Then the three of us crammed into the front seat and Lisa drove me down the block to my vehicle. I got out and we waved goodbye.

As my engine warmed up, I heard a knock on my window and looked up to see Mink. "Hey, Iris," he said once I had opened it, "your harp solo on the album sounds fabulous! I was listening to it the other day." He leaned against the car door, his voice low and tender. "It's really strong. Really strong. It sounds incredible!"

Despite my anger, it delighted me that he would say that. He had wounded me so deeply at the mixing session by suggesting that the harp might not be so important. I gleefully accepted his retraction of that idea.

"Thank you!" I chirped. "I can think about that when I'm driving home."

I set out on my way, all silly and light-headed from Mink's complimentary parting words. It was strange and not unpleasant, this subtle, belated way Mink had of apologizing. My giddiness and joy lasted for about thirty miles down the highway.

Then, like a bucket of water poured over my head, my outrage over Mink's behavior suddenly overtook me again. No danger of my falling asleep at the wheel that night; my fury kept me wide awake. Not until I reached the second rest area, two hours from Toronto, did I submit to a reluctant sleep.

* * *

"Ya, I was getting a weird vibe from Lisa that night," Mink told me the next time I saw him. "I don't think I'll go out with her anymore."

He said it lightly, as if this would be good news to me. But I thought of Lisa up in that run-down room over the Bamboo, telling me through tears about her bravery with her neck injury. I remembered her glowing like a young girl when she had heard Mink clear his throat in the stairwell. "She seemed to like you," I observed.

Mink straightened up. "Oh, she's a wonderful woman," he agreed, a bit defensively. "She'll be really good for someone, maybe even me. But not yet."

We walked past a long metal counter and into the cafeteria, where Meander Lane was to play.

"We're in there," Mink said, gesturing with his arm. "You can go find a seat. I'm gonna do the old `solitude' thing." And with that he disappeared.

As the band played that night, I noticed that Mink kept staring off, over our heads, toward the rafters of the cafeteria, as if there were someplace up there where he would rather be.

* * *

Having gotten my doctorate, finally, I moved out of the co-op and in with my mother. It was the first time I had been out of school since I was a child.

In defiance of all reason, the Meander Lane CD mail-out continued to yield dismal results. Books and magazines listing managers and record companies accumulated on my shelves. Puffy envelopes, xeroxed photos, and other assorted paraphernalia from my mailings piled up on the floor of my bedroom.

My mother and I battled constantly over the credit card debts I had amassed, from which she was obliged to rescue me. Though I regretted the predicament I had gotten us into, her moralistic attitude galled me, and I would scream back at her through tears.

To help smooth over our relationship, she paid for me to see a therapist every other week. I tried to talk to him about my group, but he would joke about rock stars dyeing their hair blue, and I knew that it was hopeless.

How strange, that my holy mission should lead to this.

* * *

Mink grabbed a fry out of my basket.

"Hey, what do you think you're doing?" I demanded in jest.

He grinned as he munched. "These aren't very good," he said.

"I like them!"

"They're all big and puffy, but they'd taste better if they were smaller and had more potato in them."

Outside the window, the lights of Yonge Street provided a colorful backdrop. Inside, Meander Lane was taking a break at the St. Louis Bar & Grill.

I removed my bulky purse from the table. "Your solo during 'Crystal and Mud'...How in the world do you do that?"

Mink eased himself into the chair next to me and then asked what I considered to be a strange question: "In my playing tonight, do you think I was too...aggressive?"

I had never known him to worry about that before. "I like it when you're aggressive."

"But was I up front too much? Do *you* think I was up front too much?" he persisted.

I smiled and pointed to the front of the stage. "I like you to be up front there as much as possible!"

Mink sighed. "I'm probably asking the wrong person. But, thanks."

A waitress came over and Mink ordered a beer. After she had

gone, Mink looked off in the direction of the entranceway for a while, eventually turning his attention back to me. "Caplan was gonna try to make it down here tonight," he said, chuckling as if embarrassed. "He's a nice guy. Very intelligent. He thinks a lot of you, you know."

Aghast that he would try to set me up with his friend, I hastened to change the subject back to Mink. "It's funny – before I knew you, I used to think that you'd be an aggressive person in real life. I thought that you were always the way you are onstage."

"I sometimes am."

"But not all the time. I thought you'd be really loud and angry. I even thought you were a violent person, just because of the way you play the guitar." As best I could, I mimicked his daunting guitar stance.

Mink laughed. "That's why I'm *not* a violent person!"

"Because you get out all your aggressions in your playing?"

He nodded.

When his beer mug arrived, Mink grabbed it off its coaster. "Cheers!" he said, clinking it against my glass before heading back toward the stage.

Caplan never did show up, for which my gratitude knew no bounds.

* * *

I arranged to get one of Meander Lane's songs on a compilation CD, at a cost of $700.00, which I billed to a credit card, of course. Whizbang Unlimited assured me that the compilation would be sent out to radio stations, managers, and record companies all over the country. Hot with anticipation, I awaited some response. None came.

One of the managers to whom I had previously sent a promotional package raved about the music, promising to shop "Upside Up" around to industry contacts, if we would pay him $5000 up front. That being impossible for us to do, he immediately lost interest in the band.

Several college and public radio stations played tracks from the Meander Lane album, and someplace in Alaska even put a couple of the songs into "heavy rotation." But no matter how many times I checked

Billboard, I never saw Meander Lane listed on any of the charts.

I got brochures in the mail about having bumperstickers, buttons, and hats made with the band logo. When I asked Danny if Meander Lane yet had a logo, he merely laughed it off as a joke.

One day, a positive review of "Upside Up" appeared in *The Ann Arbor News,* calling Meander Lane "the most pleasingly original Canadian band since Neotone."

I called Danny with the news, nearly breathless as I read the review to him over the phone.

His voice sounded uncustomarily hollow. "That's good, Iris. Why don't you try reading that to Mink? He hasn't been returning my calls lately. Maybe you'll have better luck reaching him."

* * *

"I'm house-sitting for someone," Mink informed me, rather curtly, when I did get him on the phone. "That's why people haven't been able to reach me."

"Do you have any new gigs?"

"I'll be playing with a couple of guys at Grossman's on the fifteenth."

"Any Meander Lane gigs coming up?"

"No. Nothing with Meander Lane."

* * *

Mink scratched the dog's head as we sat on the back porch steps, with a can of Molson's Canadian for each of us. Enraptured with his friend's spacious abode, he had invited me to drop by in the afternoon before the gig. "I always wanted a dog," he said. "Ruby didn't like dogs. And the place I live in now doesn't allow them. Staying here, with Nelly...it just reminds me that I need to move."

Shading my eyes from the sun, I ventured to ask: "So, is there some problem between you and Danny?"

"No, there's no problem." He petted Nelly, who was nudging at his hand. The dog rolled over and he started rubbing her belly.

"Are you gonna keep working with him?"

Ignoring my question, he continued to rub the dog's belly.

"Things are changing," he told me.

I wasn't sure I liked the sound of that. "Changing in a good way?"

Shouts of teenagers came to us from a neighbor's yard, along with the rhythmic thud of a basketball.

"I think change is almost always good," he replied.

* * *

The change, as I saw it, was that Mink went back to playing as a sideman in the endlessly shifting bands on Toronto's club scene. Why Mink would consider this a good thing mystified me.

As always, I marveled at his versatility as, in various taverns around the city, he took the stage with R&B bands, acoustic singer-songwriters (with whom he used his Gibson guitar), country warblers, urban funksters, and some of his old-time cohorts such as Eddie Noel, Wally Axel, and the ever-theatrical Delilah Zed. Intoning a witch's spell over the low pounding of a drum, Delilah once had the entire stage clouded in dry-ice smoke, while Mink, arms raised high, clapped in time to the drum beat. It was dramatic, to be sure, but had Mink left Meander Lane for this?

At one makeshift basement venue, I happened to find Mink in a small group clustered around a willowy man in a black felt hat who sat at a table in the back. Eavesdropping out of curiosity, I learned that this man was, in fact, none other than Laird Jamison, here on a brief visit from Glasgow. His voice was so soft that I could hear everyone except him. His trench coat hung loosely, like a guru's robe, and the people huddled and crouched about him only added to his exalted image. It fascinated me to see Mink, an imposing presence himself, humbly take his place among this man's followers. Overcome by a sense of my own insignificance, I drew no closer.

Danny, meanwhile, had taken to working full-time at a guitar studio, having earned a reputation as a master instrument-maker. I met him for coffee once at a place in the Beaches, and we sat at a table outside where we could view the life of Queen Street.

Danny was less than pleased with Mink. "He just sees other

people as obstacles to his career," he complained with an uncharacteristic bitterness. "Well, I'm not gonna stand in his way. Let him do what he wants, be who he wants...only, he should go by his real name, not that stupid 'Mink.'"

"What *is* his real name?" I asked.

Danny waved his hand. "I couldn't tell you that. You'd have to ask him." Looking at his watch, he gulped down the rest of his coffee. "Gotta get back to the studio, a client's coming in at twelve-thirty. Take care, you!" He pecked me on the cheek and rose to leave.

CHAPTER 18

"It sounds like me. It really sounds like *me!"* Mink repeated with childlike wonder as the song boomed through Billion Sound's mighty speakers.

At this I had to laugh. "Who else would it sound like? You're the one who's singing and playing all the instruments!"

"No," he explained, "what I mean is that I'm used to hearing Laird's voice, or Danny's, or Ruby's, or someone else's. Now it's really my voice. It's *my* thing!" He positively beamed, as if he were pregnant.

Jason had gone to the kitchen, leaving us alone to listen.

A solo guitar wailed through the fade-out. Then only the electronic buzzing of equipment filled the studio.

"Fuckin' great!" Mink exclaimed, admiring his own work without any pretense of modesty. His eyes were closed and he hummed, as if replaying the song in his mind. After several moments he stopped humming and just sat there with a Buddha-like smile. After several more moments the smile left his face. "I haven't been home much lately," he remarked, looking at me and then looking away.

"I noticed." He had been almost impossible to reach by phone over the last month. Catching him earlier that week after twenty or more failed attempts, I had learned of this session and rearranged my schedule to come.

Mink sank lower into the couch. "I have a girlfriend," he said. "I've been staying at her place most of the time. Ya, we'll be getting married in September."

It felt as if all my female parts had just been run over by a steamroller. "Who is she?" I asked.

"Her name is Emily Oscar. I don't think you've met her."

"Is she a musician?"

"No. She used to be a waitress at the Bamboo; now she works at another bar. Actually, when you see her, you might recognize her from the Bamboo."

I couldn't think of anything else to say.

Jason came back in eventually, and the two of them got caught up in their work. Mink generally ignored me for the rest of the session. Sometimes he would brush past me without seeming to notice that I was there.

Wally Axel dropped in to do some bongo parts. Brimming with good humor, he exchanged back-slaps with Mink and Jason, afterwards inviting me out to his car with the promise of a new demo tape.

"It's really rough," he apologized, handing me the boxed cassette with his illegible printing on the label, "but I hope you like it."

I wanted desperately to linger outside with him, to talk about anything...

He got into his car. "Give my love to your mom," he bid me, revving up the engine.

After he drove off, I dragged myself back towards the studio where, for once, I had no desire to be.

* * *

"Iris, this isn't uncomfortable for you, is it, meeting someone new?" Mink asked with an attempted smile.

I looked down. "No, I like your friends," I replied.

My answer appeared to please him. "My friends like you, too. In fact," he added with a chuckle, "I think my friends generally like *you* more than *me!"*

A canopy of leaves spread over us as we walked away from the pastry shop where Mink had arranged to meet me, a few blocks north of Emily's house.

"I told her all about you." Mink shot me a mischievous glance. "About your tattoo. And – she really wants to meet you."

I streetcar rumbled past, obliterating my gibberish response.

At length we arrived at one in a series of similar red brick houses on a densely-shaded residential street. Zydeco, luxuriating on the porch, jumped up and moved aside as we ascended the steps. "Goofy cat," Mink muttered, unlocking the door.

A woman in jeans and a white embroidered blouse greeted us each with a hug. Pretty in a homey way, she had merry blue eyes, blonde curls, and slightly bucked teeth.

"Iris, Emily." His introduction concluded, Mink wrapped her in a fuller embrace and kissed her lips.

In spite of what Mink had said, I doubted that I had ever seen her before. Although I had had no clear picture of what she might look like, something about her struck me as being altogether different from what I had expected.

We entered the sunny room, where a faint marijuana odor was mixed with the scent of potpourri. A tray of lemonade had already been set on a coffee table. Emily ushered me to one end of the sofa and handed me a glass. "I've never met a harpist before," she commented. "That's such a beautiful instrument! You see them in orchestras, but I imagine it's not too common."

"Not too common." I took a sip, watching the two of them settle with hands clasped at the other end of the sofa.

"Pardon the mess," Emily said, gesturing at her immaculate living room. "We have all these boxes from Mink moving in. We'll try to get them put away soon," she added, nudging Mink, who smothered her in kisses. I hadn't noticed the boxes.

As she talked on, in her pleasant, coffee-table way, about the house and the neighborhood, I began to feel like some dark, prowling thing by comparison.

At one point she moved closer to me on the sofa. "You know, we'd love to have you play the harp at our wedding, if you could. Did Mink mention that to you?"

I had been focusing on the unmistakable lilt in her voice, no doubt immensely attractive to a musician. My voice, I knew, had no such lilt. So intently was I reflecting on this that it took me a moment to absorb the meaning of her words.

When I failed to answer, she added, "I mean, if you'd like to."

I couldn't tell if this were some kind of a test. "Sure," I agreed, hoping I had gotten the answer right.

* * *

"You can get in on this side, sweetie," Emily said, pulling forward the front seat of her white Honda so that I could climb in back. Her "sweetie" grated on me. Apparently, as did Mink, she thought of me as a child.

It galled me how easily and freely they chatted on the way to the cafe, as if Mink had at last found someone with whom he could completely share himself.

Through lunch they chatted on, frequently directing their lighthearted banter toward me. Usually I just smiled and nodded.

"I used to go to a Catholic school," Emily told me, "but they didn't allow us to mix with boys, and I got fed up with that!"

She was pretty, she had a pleasant voice, she was friendly and quite nice, but nothing about her struck me as extraordinary. Why did she get to be his wife? *"You and I will NEVER be lovers!"* rang incessantly through my head; yet I didn't perceive any substantive quality she had that I was lacking. Emily hadn't been there for Mink through all these years. Had she crawled out of the woodwork just to take him from me?

After the waitress brought our food, Mink reached across the table to pinch my arm. "Eat up! Any thinner and you'd be invisible!" he quipped.

As I picked at the strange, wild-rice pudding I had ordered from the daily specials, it slowly seeped into my consciousness what it was about Emily that struck me as being so different from what I had imagined. Her age! She couldn't have been much older than I was – a year or two, if that. Possibly she was younger. *"You're a young thing, a YOUNG woman..."* I felt like the butt of some cosmic joke.

"Are you okay, Iris?" Mink asked.

I couldn't think about that right now. I would think about it later. I had to control myself. "Yeah, sure."

The pudding sat like a lumpy sponge in my mouth when I tried to swallow it.

* * *

The club had changed so much over the years that it took me a while to recognize the venue where I had first seen Mink and Ruby.

Several blocks farther west than I remembered it being, the Serpent's Plume had expanded to include the ground floor restaurant, along with an expansive back patio. Only the ancient staircase remained untouched by renovation. The bar and stage having been moved to the lower level, what those stairs led to now, God only knew.

We had arrived early so that Mink would have plenty of time to set up. His gig turned out to be a benefit for a local soup kitchen, and across the back of the stage a banner bore the slogan "FEED THE HUNGRY" in stark, black letters. I couldn't help marveling at Mink's continued commitment to so noble a cause.

"Hi, sweetie!" Emily exclaimed, embracing a lithe Hispanic woman, and at the same time making "sweetie" sound like less of a put-down. She turned to me. "Iris, this is my friend Pepita."

Pepita shook my hand, and then elbowed Mink in the ribs. "So where are you taking this lady for your honeymoon? Mexico?"

The two women burst into whoops of laughter while Mink, even in the club's dim atmosphere, appeared to turn white.

Once the players had begun to assemble, I followed Emily and Pepita to a booth near the front, where we sat down and ordered drinks. After gossiping a bit, the two of them began talking about the new band and new material that Mink would introduce that night. "Isn't that right, Iris?" Emily would ask periodically, turning to me for verification of one point or another.

In spite of the fact that I had over and over again listened to his most recent demo tape, I could think of nothing to add to their conversation.

After the soundcheck, Mink appeared at our table. "Anyone want a toke?" he asked.

Emily and Pepita rose.

"No, but can I come anyway?" I asked.

Mink shook his head. "No, we don't need any extra people."

As they left the booth and ambled off in the direction of the door, I sat there stunned. My rage built up to the point where I was actually trembling. I picked up my nearly-empty water glass and dropped it, spilling a cornucopia of ice cubes across the tabletop.

Ages passed before Mink came back. "Hey, Iris, do you want a beer or something?"

My words poured out in a shrill stream that startled me. "How-come-you-just-leave-me-here-and-go-out..."

"You didn't want any dope!" he hissed back.

"You-make-me-stay-here-and-just-leave-me..."

Without saying another word, he turned and walked away.

Comprehending nothing, I sat there motionless for several minutes before rushing to the women's washroom.

Inside the stall, my thoughts whirled into a throbbing headache. I should leave...leave...As always, this was an impossibility. In its chaotic, weakened state, my mind still recollected that this was Mink Lasher, the man before whom I had prostrated my entire being. Pettier thoughts came to me of his feeling relieved that he had chosen reasonable Emily over hysterical Iris.

I gave myself until the count of fifty to collect myself; then I left the sanctuary of the washroom to face everyone.

When I returned, Emily and Pepita were sitting next to each other in the booth, laughing at some amusing anecdote. I sat down across from them and tried to hide my eyes as well as I could behind the bottle of beer they had ordered for me.

Emily slid into the seat beside me. "Are you okay?" she asked. For an instant her eyes resembled Mink's, as if he were actually inhabiting her body. Then, once more, I became aware of her lipstick and mascara.

"Y-yeah." I was ashamed of how hideous I knew I must look after crying so hard.

She squeezed my hand, and then went back to Pepita on the other side of the table.

They both silently excused themselves when Mink came back. He nudged my arm. "Hey, you."

I glanced at him sheepishly.

"The reason I didn't want you to come out with us when we were doing pot is because it's IL-LEE-GUL! That's all it was. Okay?" He nudged me again.

I had been with him many times before when he had used marijuana, so it still wasn't clear to me why he had chosen to bar me this time, but I had no more will to argue.

"Anyway, I'm sorry." He uttered the words so softly that I almost didn't hear them.

A draft swept over me as he left the table.

Emily and Pepita soon reappeared, bubbling with conversation as if nothing had happened. But as I sat there, trying to smile along, and later as I even ventured to dance, I felt as skittish as a Halloween cat, back arched, ready to pounce on anything.

* * *

Mink eased up to Emily from behind and embraced her, folding his hands across her belly and kissing her neck. The two of them rocked gently in time to the background music under a string of colored party lights. *"Yooouuu were high,"* he crooned along with Steely Dan.

We had reassembled around our table again as the band took its second break. Pepita ordered chips and a communal pitcher of beer.

After a while Emily stretched. "Well, I could use another toke," she said, and then she turned to me. "Care to join me?" she asked.

Totally perplexed, I stood there dumbly, half expecting Mink to forbid it. When he didn't, I gave an awkward shrug and followed her toward the patio.

"It's such a heavenly night, and these places gets so stuffy..." Her lilting voice enfolded me in a warm, moist breeze as she flung open the door.

* * *

Later, at the house, Mink and Emily stood by an upstairs window, admiring the thunderstorm that had arisen in the last half hour. There was muffled laughter. I heard Mink say, "I love the way you say my name, baby-baby," although the rest of their murmurings were lost amid the beating rain.

By the time I came out of the bathroom after putting on my

pajamas, they were gone.

I crossed through the darkness and settled on the sofa-turned-bed. Still a bit shaken, I eased into perfumed sheets, feeling my body relax by degrees and then go limp. Like a heavy bassline, Mink's mantra from years before reverberated through me: *"Release it, let go, surrender..."* My heart drummed in a weird syncopation, more unsteady with each beat. Stagelights seemed to flicker across my shut eyelids. Awaiting the killer guitar solo that was sure to follow, I faded out.

* * *

So that's the story I needed to tell you.

Call it, if you want, the saga of a rock musician going from one blonde bombshell to another, as told by a mousy brunette.

Or call it a pilgrim's guide to a sacred city, although I doubt that my mecca exists on anyone else's map.

Meanwhile, I invite you to wander down Queen Street on a summer night, past the Rivoli, the Horseshoe...the air so liquid that you can drink it, so potent that it can intoxicate you with visions, drench you in legends and dreams. It can drown you.

ISBN 141200027-0

9 781412 000277